# WOODS

## SWEET GLAS

# OLLYMANDIAS

First Edition
Published by Mother Mercury
Written & illustrated by Ollymandias
Copyright © 2023 by DYM Studios
ISBN: 978-1-7396393-6-5

Photograph of Ollymandias by Lee Bowler.

www.woodshed.world • @woodshed.world • shout@woodshed.world

For Grandad.

*"There's some prat named Sue,*
*But he's got nothin' on you,*
*You are Ollymandias!"*

Δ'ΟΞΑ ΣΤΟΝ ΑΠ'ΟΛΛΩΝΑ

New Jersey

Manhattan

The Bronx

Brooklyn

Queens

Long Island

**WS** June's Crib & The Woodshed
**SH** Small Hours
**GL** Green Light Leisures
**RB** Rockaway Beach
**A** Abuela's
**SM** Stallion Motors

SH GL WS

RB

Babylon

SM

A

Ocean Parkway

NEW YORK

C. 2003

# TH3 RED PLA N3T

P. Rasnir

# Prologue

An excerpt from *The Red Planet* by Dr. P Rasnir, the Cold War scientist who founded the anarcho-communist utopia:

The plan was too transparent to work. If the air in Moscow had not been so thick with electricity, the Kremlin would have surely heard my mutiny over the static. However, with the people's pipe dream of planetary separation achieved, the limits of what could be sold as believable were rewritten. As pivotal, yet ludicrous, as the proposition was, I delivered it to the war room with neither sweat nor stutter. Playing on fears that the US would break the agreed peace and launch an attack during our departure, the council concurred that my proposal was in the greatest interest of security. So it was decided, certain factuality would not take the journey on board the people's ship, Red One. Instead, the General Secretary, his advisors, and the highest ranking military personnel would travel via an unassuming research vessel. I explained the additional defence systems designed for their ship made it a tank amongst the stars; they could fly directly into the sun without feeling a rise in temperature. This, of course, was completely false.

The old party were aware they had lost support, even within their own ranks, yet they remained oblivious to how organised the rebellion had become. Too much Russian blood had been shed for them to retain any favour; civil wars sow only sorrow as brothers kill brothers within the borders of home. Unbeknownst to the General Secretary, there was seldom a true loyalist remaining. The people still believed in communism, but their hunger for a disbandment of leadership was insurmountable. The USSR could not be allowed to barbarise the people's utopia, we could not let them land on Mars.

# ONe

Jonny looked up from the book. He felt the weight of a stare from across the train car.

"I used to know a motherfucker with the exact same face tattoo." The man said behind dark glasses.

"Yea, what's it to you?"

The man took a draw on his cigarette and smiled. "Too wild for his own good. We used to have fun though, up in the Bronx, late '70s. We were enforcers for the Screaming Eagles. Whatever was asked of us, we were willin' and able." Maintaining a fixed glare at Jonny from behind his shades, the man tapped ash onto the train floor. "I bet you're too fuckin' young to know about the S.E. Mob. Shit, back then, havin' those patches made you untouchable."

"Matta'fact, I did hear 'bout them. Ol'timers upstate like to tell stories."

"Ha, sure they do." The man turned away from Jonny for the first time and spat with the explosive stylings of a blowdart. "Sometimes I miss that motherfucker. But see, he became a liability, and there ain't space for liabilities in my line of work."

Jonny's fists tightened, he calculated the distances between himself, the man, and the door. He noted the handle's exact location on his guitar case.

"Of course, my work has changed since then. At least, *who* I work for has changed. Ease up, Jonny."

He flinched at the sound of his name from the stranger. "What you lookin' for, man?"

"Ain't lookin', kid. Tellin'." He paused, and puffed. "The letter you paid for ain't comin'. Word from our guys on Red, that's some classified shit. Your package's been seized."

"What the fuck are you talkin' 'bout?" Jonny stood up and the book dropped from his lap. "There's nothin'—"

The man rose swiftly, unsheathing a machete from his tracksuit. "They sent me specifically so you wouldn't kick up a fuss. That make sense?"

"Yup." Jonny sat down. His legs were poised like a runner on the starting block. His vision broadened and accelerated.

"Your business with the OMC is done. Finít. It won't be possible for you to communicate with the Reds again. Time to find a new girlfriend, kid."

"Le'me speak to M, this gotta be a misunderstandin'."

The man slid open the door to the next carriage, weapon concealed, and paused. "Hear me, don't get above yourself. You no longer know who M is."

"Fuck." His gaze dropped to the battered book on the ground. Ava had lent it to him in the weeks that lead up to leaving, he had read it ten times over. The distance between them caved in on him; for the past three years, exchanging letters had been the only window to her world. His chest tightened while thundering thoughts flashed with what she could've of been trying to say.

Jonny snapped back when the train arrived at First Ave. He grabbed the book, tucked it into the waistband of his cut-off jeans, and left the station in a daze. He stopped on the nearest corner, propped up his guitar, and patted down his pockets. Bent and beat, he found the business card marked 'Ormen Moving Company'. He flipped open his phone and called the number. Straight dial tone. He kept walking, taking a detour past Blazin' Eights, the bar where he paid M for Ava's letter two weeks prior. Poking his head in, he hoped to spot a mop of fiery hair in one of the shadowed booths. No dice, just stubbly men at the bar, and a couple with their backs to him at the pool table.

Jonny didn't hear his name called as he walked past Tompkins Square Park. His feet continued on autopilot. A block away from work, he felt a hand on his shoulder. He spun round and slapped blindly. The ball of his palm connected in a crack against silky hair. A red hat took flight, and the body dropped.

"Kiwi? Shit!" Jonny dropped his guitar and darted to his friend face down on the floor. "Bro, I'm so sorry!" He said, grabbing Kiwi's arm and lifting him to sit up.

Wide-eyed and dumbfound, Kiwi looked at Jonny, blood dripping from a graze above his brow. "What the fuck dude?!"

"Shit, man. Le'me help you up. I'm so fuckin' sorry."

"Dude, what?"

"Look at me. Can you see straight?"

"Er, yea. I'm okay." He said, regaining his composure. "Bit bloody rattled, mate, but I'll get on. Shit."

"Bro, I can't—fuck. I'm so sorry."

"You're alright, come le's hav'a lil' sit down. Where's me hat?"

The pair took a seat in Tompkins, and Kiwi lit a spliff retrieved from the inner brim of his bucket hat.

"Why'd you slap me, mate?"

"Bro, I hate people comin' up behind me. I don't know, it's been a weird day, I'm sorry."

"Quit apologisin', drongo! Na, I mean why a slap?"

"Word. Well I'm 'bouta head into work. Ain't gonna risk a bust knuckle."

"Oh, cool. Yea, I'd hate to've hurt ya hand with my fuckin' jawline."

"You sure you a'ight?"

"Yeamate, I eat concrete for breakfast. I'll clean it up and put some ice on there at the restaurant."

Kiwi passed the joint, Jonny took a toke, and coughed up a lung.

"What the fuck is this?"

"Too much for ya, boyo?"

"Hell no, this shit taste like lawn clippin's. How are we friends and this is what you're smokin'?"

"June won't fuckin' sell to me, man. On account of how *aggressively heterosexual* I am."

"She said that?"

"Summin' of the sort. I think it jus' scares her how attractive she secretly finds me."

"Okay, yea, that right there. Tha's why she doesn't fuck wit'you."

"It's her loss."

"Nope, it's your loss. She has the best weed on the East Coast, and you're smokin' this reginald regularis bush crap."

"So let me buy some off you."

"Na, ya crazy, she finds out everything. You ain't worth the risk."

"Well I'm waitin' on my guy now. Come, talk to him, see if he could use a new supplier."

"Huh, a'ight. Not a bad idea. This guy's gotta be a fuckin' hermit to not already be sellin' her shit."

"Speak of the devil, there he is."


Suede fringe and double-wide denim flares caught the wind as the dude approached. His mop of hair was longer and curlier than Kiwi's, but his sunburnt forehead was winning a war to expand its territory.

"SK!"

"Ay, my man. How you doin' Jonny?"

"Maintainin'. Lookin' forward to playin' tonight."

"Right on."

"Wait, you guys know each other?"

Jonny and SK looked at Kiwi.

"We both in the Small Hours band, numbnuts. Ain't you seen the show?"

"Aw, no way! Thought I recognised you from somewhere, but could never place it."

Jonny scoffed. "How the fuck you not put that together, bro? You ever seen another goatee with that many angles involved?"

"Bet it's the stupid monkey suit, man. Those god forsaken frills seriously bring down the Sax Killer vibe."

"Yea, nah, yea, mate. Now you say it, I do feel a tad silly. But anyway, SK's my ol'faithful ganja man."

"Hm."

"So what can I do you for, Kiwi?"

"A zip of your finest, please."

"Sure thing, that'll be four-fifty, brother dude."

SK pulled a doughnut box out of his dufflebag, which elicited a sceptical side-eye from Jonny, and the cash passed hands without being seen.

"Pleasure doin' business, as always." Kiwi said, smelling the seam of the doughnut box.

"Talking of the terror that is our velvet tuxedos, you convince the boss to let you make that alteration?"

Jonny let slip a sly smile. "Yup, chimney twins gonna have it ready for me Monday."

"Ah, killer! It's gonna look horrendous." SK laughed.

"What you gettin' goin' Jonboy?" Kiwi asked.

"Shorts. Gettin' the trousers chopped at the knee."

"What a look! Should've guessed it, ay."

Kiwi and SK began the decent into small talk, but Jonny grew quickly distant from the conversation.

"Yo, Kiwi. You got minutes on your cell?" He interrupted.

"Er, should do."

"Mind if I make a phone call right quick?"

Kiwi passed him the clam. "Long as it's local, cunt."

"No doubt. Watch this please?" Jonny left them with his guitar and walked out of earshot. He dialled the number for Ormen Moving Company. It rang.

"Hello?" An unmistakable, mildly Russian, strikingly sinister voice answered the call.

"M. We need'a talk."

"Who is this?"

"Jonny Vulcain, you just had one of your goons confront me on the train."

"Ah, well I'm disappointed it didn't instil the intended message. Your business with us is done, do not pursue this further or there

will be irreversible repercussions."

"I need you to tell me why Ava's letter got pulled!"

"You are in no position to demand anything! I made it very clear when you opened this line of communication that there was to be no leaking of classified information. That term was broken immediately."

"Not by me! I paid you the stellafax fee, if it didn't fly, let her send another."

"She will not be sending any more letters. We are the only herald operating at this point, and Ms. Igwe has proven herself a liability. We will not allow her any form of off-planet communication."

"This is bull–"

"Do not call again. If you continue to make noise, you will be deemed an official threat to security, and that is a greenlight that you do *not* want. You met my associate Cain under strict orders not to harm you, believe me, without such restrictions his methods will be *more* than unpleasant."

"I jus'–"

Dial tone.

"Fuck!" He froze, fists clenched.


"Thanks, dude."

Kiwi took his phone back. "No sweat, you good?"

"Yea. We should head up to the studio." Jonny said, grabbing his guitar case.

"Let's boogie." SK said with a rolling shoulder shake.

"Catch ya later, Kiwi. Sorry again."

"All bless, boyo." He gripped Jonny's hand and pulled him close. "Big love, Hurricane."


Jonny and SK walked across the street and buzzed into the building.

"We gotta talk, dude. That bud you're sellin' is garbage, no offense."

"You think?"

"Oh yea, I know. And for four-fifty an ounce, you *wylin'*. Le'me get you right."

"What you got in mind?"

"My homegirl June, I'll put you in contact. Top shelf bud, at a better price than what you get now, no brainer."

"Okay, sweet deal. She deliver?"

"Yea, but only orders above a pound. If you need smaller, you can get it from one of her workers, she has one uptown you could hoffa at."

"I can dig that. Thanks, Jonny. Never knew you're in the game."

"I'm not, jus' family affiliated."

Before the elevator doors opened to the studio, Vinnie's voiced boomed behind the metal. "You cheeky fuckin' bastard! I got 'alf a mind to string ya up by yer sodden mouldy mop strings!"

# Two

Sherm's concentration drifted away from his swampocalyptic fantasy novel when the woman sat across from him began singing.

"I had no choice, but to hear you." Her eyes were closed, lined with black wings, and grazed with glitter. Pink hair fell around a large pair of headphones. She sang to herself, with a bedroom confidence, as if she forgot she was riding the subway. "You treat me like, I'm a princess. I'm not used to, liking tha-a-at."

Sherm softened as he listened, his eyes smiled behind thick frames as he watched her, captivated by every knit of her brow and each anticipated breath.

"You've already won me o-ver-er!"

When the chorus hit, he recognised the song, June played this album on occasion. It was Alanis Morissette. The girl sang it well, in tune, with energy. He continued to admire her, enjoying the performance, and taking in all the subtle expressions that formed the sum of her allure. Floral tattoos adorned porcelain skin, bright and colourful, bold yet delicate. She wore a spiked leather choker and semi-precious stones set in stirling rings.

"Your love is thick, and it swallowed me whole."

Sherm felt himself warm. Erotic images entered his head. He averted his gaze to the list of subway stations above, still focused on the sound of her voice. The train had been sat at Bedford for

a few minutes, he dreaded it pulling away from the platform, the next stop was his destination.

*Stand clear of the closing doors, please. Bing-bong.*

Sherm winced.

"Don't be surprised if I love you, for all that you are!" As she closed out the second chorus, and the train picked up speed, her body bubbled and she opened her eyes.

Jumping on the break in the song, Sherm beamed at her and offered a solitary round of applause. His kind smile was infectious and she reflected it back to him.

"Hey, thank you." She said, removing her headphones.

"You have an awesome voice." He gestured to the empty seat next to her. "Do you mind?"

"Not at all."

Sherm relocated and offered a gentle hand. "I'm Sherm."

"Kate, nice to meet you."

"Sorry if this is too forward, but, er—I'm getting off at the next station. Do think I could maybe get your number? I work with musicians and I really enjoyed your singing, I'd love to talk with you sometime."

"Oh really? Well, I don't have a cell phone, but I'm getting off at First Ave too. We could get a drink now, if you want?"

"Okay, sweet! Um, I need to be at work soon. One drink will be okay, though. Yeah, let's do it."

"Cool, I have to stop by the bar I work at to pick something up, we can hang there. You know Blazin' Eights?"

"Yeah, that's across the street from where I'm going. Perfect."

Sherm followed Kate off the train and through the turnstile. He was momentarily lost in watching her push against the barrier with her waist, hypnotised by her hips. He pictured her daisy dukes being pulled down over her fishnetted legs, but was swiftly brought back to the present when she span round.

"So what is it that you do?"

"I, er, work at a talk show. You heard of Small Hours?"

"Hell yea! The late slash early show, that's sick! Vinnie Cliff drinks at the bar now and then, and I actually met someone else

11

who works there a couple weeks ago, the guitarist dude."

"Jonny?"

"Yea, that's him."

"Get outta here, he's my best friend!"

"Wow, small world."

"Smaller city. How'd you meet him?"

"At the bar, he just stopped by for a minute, but I recognised him from a Bad Dead gig the night before."

"Right on, yeah, that's his favourite band."

"Mine too. I really love the direction the house band have taken since Jonny joined, he goes hard. I'd like to meet him again sometime."

"Well, if you want, come by the studio after our drink. You can watch the show get filmed."

"That would be insane, ah, I'm so glad we met!"

"Same here." He smiled at her, and when she smiled back, he blushed a strong shade of rose. "Are you from the city?"

"Nah, White Plains. Moved to Queens a few years ago."

"Word, well I won't hold it against you."

"Ha, it's not that bad. I take it you're a real New Yorker, then?"

"Yup, Greenpoint, born and raised."

"Nice, you must be doin' pretty well for yourself."

"Well, I still live with my moms."

"Mamma's boy, huh? I won't hold that against you. She seems to have raised a sweet kid."

"Thanks, moms plural, actually."

"Cute. You're Jewish?"

"Well done, detective. Very much so, that is, until the question of religion gets involved."

"Two Jewish mothers? That sounds intense."

"Hm, stereotypical, slightly anti-semetic. But yeah, overbearingly intense at points. Incredibly well-stocked fridge though."

"Ha, I'm sorry, just fuckin' with you."

"You're good."

"So what exactly do you do at Small Hours?"

"This and that, help where it's needed. I got Jonny the job there, my aim is to be talent scouting, bringing underground acts to the show. Break some bands."

"Right on."

"What I really wanna get into is artist management. I know I could do big things, but I haven't found the right opportunity yet. That's why I wanted to speak with you, actually. You take singing seriously?"

"Hardly, I enjoy it, but I'm not like, pursuing a career."

"Maybe you could. Get some musicians to back you up, or even a DJ—you write at all?"

"Ha, you have an imagination. I guess I write. Silly little poems, really."

"Would you be interested in trying them out over music? Or maybe just playing around with some covers? I'm sure I could get Jonny to workshop a song or two with you."

"Huh, I don't know about sharing my writing. I'd be down to fuck aroun' something with Jonny though. You could make that happen?"

"Um, probably, yeah."

"Do you manage him?"

"I'd like to, but no. He wants to move to The Red Planet in a couple years, so, he's not got much interest in a musical career."

"He wants to live with the space communists?!"

"Yeah, he was meant to go with his girlfriend in 2000, but missed the shuttle."

"Word, okay. How did they manage that?"

"It's a long story, but they didn't, just him. She's up there now, working as a biomedical engineer."

"That's gnarly. Are they still together?"

"Yeah."

"Hm. I heard it's a pretty decent life for creative types, looked after by the state and that, no such thing as a starvin' artist."

"Everyone's looked after, supposedly."

"Yea, that's *if* you're selected to go. Isn't it impossible to get a place these days for anyone who isn't a scientist?"

Sherm shrugged. "He's already been accepted. I don't really wanna talk about it though, the thought of him leaving freaks me out."

"Copy, no doubt."

When they reached Blazin' Eights, Kate introduced Sherm to the bartender, took two bottles of beer from the fridge, and poured two shots of Irish whiskey.

"Fancy a game of pool?"

"You're on, thank you."

They cheersed and necked the whiskey.

"So what do you do for fun?" Kate asked while she racked up the table.

"Um, I skate. Hang out. Have a couple hobbies. I'm pretty into tabletop games."

"Like Monopoly?" She rolled the triangle into place and span the eight ball as she dropped it into the center.

"Fuck no. I play Masters of Mojo, mainly. It's a card game, and a miniature wargame."

"Miniature *war*game?"

"Basically, you assemble squads of miniature models, roll dice, and use stratagey to destroy your opponent."

"Okay, like toy soldiers. You wanna break?"

"No, you go ahead. And it's more complicated than that."

Kate swigged her beer, lined up her shot, and bam! The balls reached every corner of the table, two stripes finding a pocket. "Nice. So enlighten me."

"First thing is building the models, you buy each character, and they come as separate parts. It makes a big difference what weapons and equipment you give them. Then you have to paint them."

Kate nailed another stripe. "How do you paint them?"

"With a small brush, attention to detail, and in my case, a lot of cannabis."

"That's cool." She bent over the table in front of Sherm.

"Yeah. It is." His glasses fogged a little.

Her shirt rode up and part of a large snake tattoo was exposed. The scales followed the dip of her back and disappeared into the waistline of her shorts. Bam! She blasted the cue ball, catching

14

the edge of a stripe, and sending it sideways to its destination. "And so you have your painted miniatures?"

"Um, yeah. Nice shot. You, er, get together a team of minis, and set them up on a table of terrain. It's not like a traditional gameboard, with spaces or squares, it's meant to look like a scaled down battlefield. Masters of Mojo is all set in a post-apocalyptic swamp land. Most people build and paint their own terrain too."

"This sounds so involved." She knocked out one more stripe, but left herself without any possible shots. "Dammit." She missed an impossible shot and passed the cue to Sherm.

"Thanks. It is, but that's half the fun. Painting minis is like therapy for me, it's so meditative. Throw on an audiobook, or good album, and nothing else exists in the world." Sherm drove home an easy solid, and lined up a long shot.

"Word, I see the appeal in that. But how do you play the game, how do you win?"

Sherm's geometry was off. "Eurgh. It comes down to your choices, really, and the will of the dice gods. In short, you take turns making tactical decisions, and roll a set of dice to see how successful they were. You're commanding an army for domination of the bayou."

"You're like, a serious nerd, it's cute." Another stripe eliminated. She looked up at Sherm from across the table.

His eyes moved quickly to meet hers, he feared she noticed them lingering. "Hm, thank you?"

"It was a compliment." She smiled, and rotated to take her next shot.

"You're really kicking my ass at this."

"Oh yeah, don't feel bad. This is *my* playtime escapism." The final stripe left the felt. "Corner pocket." She tapped the table's nearest corner with the back end of her pool cue. Off the cushion and across the table, the eight ball rolled to conclusion. "Good game." She curtseyed.

"Wow, yeah, for you it was. I'm swimming back to land, there's a shark in the water."

"Ha, that was lame, but thanks. Step outside with me for a cig?"

15

"Of course."

Sherm was quick to offer a flame when Kate placed a cigarette between her lips. "You have beautiful eyes." He said, while lighting her smoke.

She inhaled and pulled away. "Thanks."

Sherm tapped his booge atop the pack three times. "We should probably head over after this. That cool with you?"

"Yeah, sure. I'm excited, never been to a TV studio before."

"It's funky, but there can be a lot of waiting around at points. If things aren't too rushed tonight, I'll give you a tour of the whole place."

"Sweet, I'd like that. So are you kinda a big shot round there?"

"Hardly."

"Well you look like you know what you're doin', sharp dresser."

"Ha, thanks, I try. And, I mean, I do know what I'm doing. But, honestly, I'm kinda low on the ladder."

"Ah, fake it 'till ya make it."

"Type shit."

"How old are you, Sherm?"

"Twenty-one."

"Hm, you're gonna do just fine, give it time."

"You mind if I ask how old you are?"

"Twenny-two, born in eighty-one."

"Oh, so we're like the same age. I kinda felt you were a few years older than me."

"How old did you think I was?"

"I don't know, nothing past twenty-five. You just have this confidence about you, like you got some experience under your belt."

"Are you callin' me a slut? You think I'm easy?"

"No! God, no! I'm sorry, that really came out wrong. I just mean—"

"Calm down, I'm fuckin' with you. I know that's not what you meant."

"Okay, shit. That one got me going." Sherm visually took steps to slow his breath, looking straight up at the sky.

"You're funny." Kate took a drag. "*Experienced*, I'll remember that one."

They moseyed across Tompkins Square Park towards the Small Hours studio, the large ring of keys strapped to Sherms hip jingled as they strolled. Each time she laughed, his ears warmed, and a chill raced under his skin. With every step that brought them closer to the park's edge, he slowed their pace.

"You don't wanna go to work, huh?"

"Na, it's just—" Sherm blinked fast. "I'm enjoying your company."

"Me too. But I'll be honest, I can't *stand* walking slow."

"Oh, fair. Well, we're basically there. Let's get it steppin'." Sherm set off in a comically fast speedwalk. "C'mon, keep up!"

Kate near enough jogged to follow him across the street, giggling behind him. "You're an idiot, ha! I love it."

When the elevator doors opened out onto the studio floor, Kate gazed around the room. "This is cool."

"Uh-huh, can you just wait right here for a second? I need to speak to Vinnie real quick, then I can give you the grand tour."

"No problem."

Sherm made his way behind the stage curtains to the boss's office, he took a sharp deep breath, and knocked.

"G'won!"

Sherm opened the door. "Hi, Miste—"

"Oh for fucksake! The bloody moppin' wombat's back, and christ alive, he's got the gaul'a wear a collard shirt again! I told'ya, I need my janitor a'look like a janitor, put yer greys on, boy."

"Er, sorry, Mr. Cliff. That's actually what I wanted to speak with you about. I was hoping, just this once, you maybe wouldn't make me change into the overalls?"

"N'why on'erth would that be?"

"Well, I've brought someone to see the show, a singer. I'd, er— I'd rather look professional tonight."

Vinnie's brow coiled.

"But of course I'll still take care of everything! I can scrub and mop just as efficiently wearing a shirt, I promise."

"Take me'a meet'er."

"You—you want to meet her?"

Vinnie was off out the office. Sherm followed in his wake. They reached Kate by the bleachers alarmingly fast.

"Kate—this is, er, Kate. Kate, er, Mr. Cliff. Sir."

"Nice t'meet ya. So you're a singer, ay?"

"Hi, we've met before, actually. And—um, I wouldn't really call myself a singer, no."

"Uh, 'ear that, Sherm? Not a singer. Interestin'."

"She's talented! I heard her singing on the subway."

"Do you know, Kate, what it is that Sherm does 'ere?"

"Not exactly, maybe assistant producer or some shit."

"Assistant producer, 'uh. Maybe in'a poor boy's dreams, 'e's the fuckin' caretaker! 'E cleans the blommin' pisser!"

"Sir! I never said—"

"Disappointed I am, Sherm. It would seem you been feedin' me little porkie pies, son. Weave me a narrative in meager 'opes a'gettin' yer todger wet!"

"No, sir! Er—pork, sir?"

"You cheeky fuckin' bastard! I got 'alf a mind to string ya up by yer sodden mouldy mop strings!"


CLANK. Elevator doors opened on to the situation and the pilots took one breath of the atmosphere.

"Nope." SK said, and the doors closed, taking him and Jonny back down to Earth.

"I think I should probably go." Kate said.

"You're more than welcome t'stay n'watch the show, darlin'. But think twice 'bout leavin' with *this* scoundrel."

"I—"

"You, Sherman. 'Ubris will be your downfall, your job ain'ta scout for talent, it'sa sweep the floors. Unless it's the bloody Bully followin' you out them lift doors, don't bring another person t'this studio."

"I'm sorry, Kate. I shouldn't have brought you into this."

18

"You shouldn't 'ave lied 'bout your position! That Oxford collar puts your neck above it's station, boy. Go change int' uniform, now!"

"It's okay, well, I mean *this* isn't okay." She said, gesturing circularly towards Vinnie. "But don't sweat it. I'll see ya 'round, Sherm."

Sherm's shoulders rolled inward as Kate walked to the elevator. Vinnie yelled one more thing about a uniform and darted off. The studio workers returned to whatever they were focused on before the upset, or at least pretended to look busy. Sherm moved through the buzz and backstage. There lay a long hallway of doors behind the curtain. One locked door was marked SUPPLIES. The keyring on Sherm's hip held at least two-dozen keys; one key stood out, it had been recut onto a custom shaped blank. Sherm turned the skull-faced key and flicked on the lightbulb. The room was small, stocked up with cleaning gear, and immaculately organised. On the edge of a shelf holding a hundred jaycloths hung grey overalls with "Sherm" embroidered on a white and red patch. In the far corner there was a modest desk, clipped to it a lamp, on one side a wooden chest. Sherm locked the door and took a seat at his table.

"That happened so fucking fast." He sat with his head in his hands. "What the fuck?"

When a teardrop stained his khakis, he bolted upright and reached for his hip. The smallest key on his person opened the chest. Inside was a personal cassette player, tiny paint pots, brushes, tupperware container, and a miniature model. Sherm klunked the button that brought to life an Ethiopian jazz tape, laid the painting gear on the table, and grabbed a jar of water from the shelving rack next to him. He found the paint in the tupperware still wet when he cracked open his makeshift palette. The light of the desk lamp was cool and bright, showing every detail of the half-finished model. Sherm turned the character in his hand and paid attention to his breath, slowing its pace to match the rhythm of his premeditated emergency respite.

# THRee

"*Epistemological supra-disciplinarity*? ¿Qué diablos?" The book slammed shut under it's own academic weight, and June fell backward into a dark pillow abysm. She uncrossed her legs and raised them up parallel with the metal posts of her bedframe. Laying with her hands in support of outstretched knees, she felt a tightness run through her thighs. As her muscles eased, and mind reset, she swung her legs down reverting to an upright position. "Mañana." She concluded, collecting the array of books and handwritten notes that covered her satin sheets, stacking them on the dresser opposite. She stood on her toes and raised her arms to touch the low basement ceiling. Pushing back against her fingers, June elongated herself to full extension and inhaled.

Her CD player made a reading-whir as she climbed back into bed holding a xeroxed zine and magic wand. The wand plugged into the wall behind her nightstand, and warm synth sounds rose from the ovular boombox adjacent. June perused the photocopied pages, skipping over think-piece articles and agony-aunt features, as the music kicked to life with gothic guitar riffs and theatrical lyrics of graveyard scenes. She lingered on a collection of explicit femme fatal photographs, but flicked further forward to land on the publication's erotic horoscopes.

Virgos el año entero se sentirá de fiesta vas a comer mucho 'bizcocho'. Si sabes a lo que me refiero. ¿De hecho, sabes de 'sploshing'? La práctica de juegos eróticos con comida. Sé que puede sonar, digamos raro, para une virgo más primero aceptemos que te encantaría probar algo diferente y si alguien puede mantener las cosas en orden y con placer a la vez eres tu. A mi me encanta la miel tibia y las frutas frías poco a poco, lamida a lamida, mordisco a mordisco, aquí y haya en algunos momentos de mi intimidad. ¿Qué te gustaría saborear mientras te saborean? Lo importante es que disfrute tu paladar.

The wand rumbled under the duvet, and June lost focus on the words. As she teetered on the edge of escaping her head, a loud klunk broke the spell.

"I don't know, man." the apartment door opened. "I think you should just go to the bar tomorrow." Jonny's voice carried from the hallway through the bedroom walls.

"¡Bastados!" June exclaimed in hushed breath.

"It's embarrassing, bro!" Sherm said, entering the kitchen-slash-living area outside her door.

She clicked off the gatling-gun vibration, and flung off the covers, inadvertently yanking hard on the wand's cable. The taut wire jerked the bedside table, and threw down her cup of herbal tea, sending violent shards of porcelain flying across the rug.

"Fuck!"

"You alright, June?" Sherm called

"Yea! Jus' a minute!" June stood, shut her eyes, and sharply exhaled through her nose. She picked up the fragments of mug, grateful that it broke rather than shattered, and really grateful that it had already been drunk. She put the broken pieces and soggy teabag back in what remained of the vessel, and left her room.

"Hola, all good. I dropped my tea. What is embarrassing?"

"Word, hey. Er, I messed it up with this really cool girl today."

"You didn't mess it up, Vinnie did." Jonny said as he entered from his room, offering June a casual salute, and dropping a stack of cards on the kitchen table.

Sherm washed his hands and slumped into one of the dining chairs. "He fucking screamed at me, over nothing, just snapped. Like, it was all going so well, then it all went really shit."

June dropped the broken crockery in the bin and proceeded to wash her hands once the sink was free. "Sorry, man. That sounds rough. You know where to find her?"

"Yeah, she works at a bar on Tompkins, but I can't go in there. I just feel humiliated."

"Dude, if she changes her mind about you because of someone else's opinion, she ain't worth the heartache."

"Jonny is right." June filled the kettle. "You guys want a tea?"

"I'm straight." Jonny said, taking two tins of beer out of the fridge.

"And me." Sherm said taking the beer that was offered to him. "Maybe you're right Jonny, but imagine I walk into the bar and she starts laughing, or what if everyone starts laughing. She told them all the tall tale of a sad-sack janitor that lost his dignity to a live studio audience."

"This is gonna be on the show?"

"No, it was early in the night, but everyone I work with saw it go down."

"Jonny saw?"

"Yeah. Wait, you didn't address the laughing thing, you think that's a possibility?"

"I don't know, I didn't see what happened, and I don't know how mean she is."

"That's so not reassuring!"

"Sorry. I hope she won't joke about it, but people tell stories."

Jonny sat opposite Sherm whose face was now resignedly planted on the table.

"You saw this go down, Jonny, and didn't say something?"

"Huh, the Vinnie thing? What could I have done?"

"Stepped in?"

Sherm sat up. "Not that I expect you to always save me, but I did feel weird that you just left, bro."

"You fucking left?!"

"Woah, you're comin' in mighty hot right now. It's a yes-no situation."

"How so?"

"I was in the elevator, doors open, fan's spinnin' shit everywhere. SK made an executive decision and hit the first floor button."

"SK hit the button?" Sherm asked.

"Yeaman, I should've moved quicker, but I wasn't thinkin' straight. My bad."

"All good, I'm glad to know it wasn't an intentional abandonment."

"Sorry for raising my voice."

"No sweat."

"You guys playing your card game?"

"Yup, bit'a Mojo just what Sherm needs to get his head right." Jonny started construction on a spliff behind his wall of trading cards.

"You're not wearin' makeup tonight?" June asked him.

"Na! I told River I hate havin' to wash my face before bed, so they offered to take it off when we wrap."

"That's nice of them. But you should really wash your face either way."

"That's what they said."

"It's a shame though, I like seeing you all dolled up!"

"He secretly likes it too." Sherm said rooting through his backpack.

"I don't mind, gettin' used to it. But takin' it off sucks. Eyes all stingin' n'shit, makes 'em double bloodshot."

"Sounds like you are doin' it wrong."

"Probably, ain't nobody given me makeup lessons before."

"Have you got any leftovers going, June?" Sherm asked.

"Nope, no food today."

"Too bad, I could've really gone for some toast-o-knees."

"You mean tostones. Sorry, kitchen's closed."

"There's no hot pockets or something quick I could make?"

"Leave it out, Germ." Jonny interjected. "We bouta play, you can't go make yaself a meal right now, focus up."

June stirred her tea and headed to the crush pink couch. She picked up a motoring magazine and a half-smoked spliff from coffee table.

"What are you getting into?" Sherm asked her.

"I'm shopping for a car, or a van, I think a van."

"You selling the bike?"

"No way, adding to the collection. My bike is perfect, but sometimes you need more seats, d'you know?"

"Are we going on a road trip?"

"Maybe! I want to stop being such a hermit. The only things I leave the house for are work, school, and visiting Abuela. Sure, I go to the bar now and then, but *us three* never do anything. We need more adventures outside the apartment. So I've been thinking, I should get a car."

"Right on, Bug." Jonny said, slightly singeing his index finger and thumb in the process of toasting a fronto leaf.

"Then I thought, no. I should get a van."

"Jheeze, a family van would be awesome!" Sherm said before spitting beer from his nose in a small spluttering fit. "Urgh."

"You okay?"

"Yeah, just got a bit excited about the van plan."

"Okay, well don't do that when I get one, or you'll be banned from the van."

"Copy that, I'll behave." He said regaining composure behind red-rosey cheeks.

"I'm having a hard time looking though, it needs to be the *right* van."

"What are your parameters for that?"

"Well, obviously you know my bike, it's glitter-sparkle purple, pure pussy power."

"Accurate description."

"Mm."

"So my standards are high. I don't want a van that has no life. I want a van that makes me smile."

"Some va-va-vroom, as the French might say."

"If you say. But I haven't found one, they all look like an Arkansas nuclear vacation, or like the owner enjoys hard boiled sweets and hands them out at school gates."

"Vivid."

"It's going to be good. I will find one, and it will drive me away from my cozy-zone, in leather seated comfort."

"Do the seats need to be leather? They get so gross in the summer, sticky-city-central."

"Yes, Sherm. The seats need to be leather, black leather."

"It needs a good sound system."

"Sí, Jonny, that's on the list."

"Why don't you just get a standard van and upgrade it?"

"I might have to, but it would be so nice to just meet one that's already perfect."

"Yo, this reminds me. Can you give me a ride to the Lower tomorrow? The L ain't runnin'."

"What time? I'm goin' into the city at noon for deliveries, but then out to Abuela's round three."

"That's perfect. I shouldn't be long, so maybe you can bring me back too?"

"Sure, just be ready to go on my time."

"Yessir."

"You left something at the studio, bro?"

"Na, I'm goin' to Charlie's uncle's gym."

"What? Why?"

"I feel like I should check in with Avir. See how he's doin'."

"Word. That's good of you. Honestly, I'd be terrified to show my face around there."

"Yea, I ain't exactly lookin' forward to it."

"Who's Avir?"

"Charlie's older brother."

"Oh, he's the boxer?"

"Yup."

"What are you going to say?"

"I don't know. Nothing about that night. I just wanna see that he's okay. Charlie did a lot for the big guy."

"He did. Always fighting Avir's corner."

They sat reflective for a few seconds.

A sly smile rose across Jonny's face. "Remember the bathroom brawl?"

Sherm snapped back from wherever he had been. "Are you crazy? *Of course!*"

"What happened?" June asked.

"You don't know?" Shem's eyes narrowed. "This was back in Sixth grade. The day after Avir had his first amateur fight."

"Oh, I remember you guys going to that! Didn't you get grounded for being out so late?" She said to Sherm.

"I did! *Totally* worth it. The fight was a big deal at school, they even included it in morning announcements, Avir graduated from there a year before. But anyway, it was lunchtime, and the three of us are in the toilets, sharing a cigarette. Then like four or five kids from our class walk in, making fun of Avir."

"Because he's autistic?"

"Exactly. They were doing some stupid impression of him like it was a post-fight interview."

"Eurgh, huele bichos."

"Man, I hated those clowns." Jonny grimmaced. "There were five of 'em."

"Word, that's right, five of these fucks, standing round, laughing. I'll never forget what happened next. Charlie doesn't even blink, he runs to the one in the middle and clocks him right on the chin!"

"Bang! No hesitation. Guy's *twice* his size."

"Charlie was always the guy to break up a fight, turns out he could throw a mean punch! The kid crumples, and Charlie hits another one in the gut."

"Then shit got hectic."

"Charlie gets that one in a headlock, now they're wrestling on the floor. That leaves three fuckheads and us two."

"So what d'you do?"

"Sherm got knocked the fuck out."

"Hey! He broke my glasses, I didn't black out."

"A ref could'a counted to ten before you got up, no offense."

"Okay, so my nose was bleeding, a lot. But then *this* guy—eurgh, I don't even wanna big you up after that comment, you're so annoying."

"Hehe, tell her what happened, Germ."

"Jonny fucking exploded, in a storm of fists and kicks, he was spinning round like the Tasmanian Devil in a kung-fu movie!"

"What? *This* Jonny?"

"Yeah, who knew? He's flying at these kids like a freaking tornado."

"I jus' le'my lizard instinct take the wheel."

"It was wild, but all over fairly quick. A teacher walked in hearing the rumble, and we all got sent to the principle's office."

"You get in trouble?"

"Not even! Turns out the principle has an autistic daughter, and she was so proud of Avir being an alumni, that when we explained why we were fighting, she let the three of us go, not so much as a phone call home."

"Wow."

"Mm."

"And that, June, was the epic event that spawned Jonny's legendary nickname."

"The Hurricane?"

"The mother fucking Hurricane."

"Big up Charlie for that one, man. Nobody fucked with The Three Blunters after word went round 'bout what went down."

"The Three Blunters forever, dude." Sherm wiped steam from his lenses, and rubbed his eyes on a shirt sleeve. "Okay, we're playing Mojo now, I can't deal with any more storytime. That spliff ready yet?"

Jonny licked closed his creation, compacted it, and put it to flame. "We here."

"You told that well, Sherm, enjoy your nerd game."

"Um, it's pretty cool. But thanks, good luck with the van search."

June turned on the rest of her spliff and proceeded to peruse the pages for a future chariot. Jonny and Sherm took turns drawing cards, casting spells, and rolling dice. The basement became engulfed in a haze of smoke, and they each forgot themselves.

Making snap judgements over an endless stream of thumbnail images was oddly stimulating. It felt utterly mindless, and yet captivated her entire attention. The din of internal monologue was hushed, with the exception of that which pertained to picturing herself owning each vehicle. Each page proposed a couple dozen potential options, many of which her eyes scrolled past in a fraction of a second, but some drove off with her imagination. She envisioned herself in the driver's seat, new wave music blaring, windows down on an open road. None of the vans felt right, but she lived a hundred fleeting lives in those pages, and she was glad to escape her head.

"I've got you now, Jonny! With my Alligator Gladiator activated, you don't stand a goddamn chance."

The kitchen table's excitement level had risen to an unignorable level and June couldn't help but cock an ear to listen in.

"Hm, that's what you think, yea?" Jonny took a card from his hand and slammed it down on the table. "I play, Jonny Vulcain, the Guitar Wieldin' Hurricane."

"Dude! What the fuck? I told you before, I'm not playing with cards you made yourself!"

"Why? It's a good card, man."

"Yeah, *way* too fucking good!"

June's interest was now firmly sparked. "You made a Jonny card?"

"Yea, and Sherm's all bent outta shape 'bout it."

"Show me."

Jonny passed her the hand drawn card.

"It's really cool man, I *get* it, but it just doesn't work in the game! First off, every card needs to be balanced, Mojo operates on delicate numeric formulas! You set the power *way* too high and it breaks the mechanics. Neither of us are good enough at math to create new cards."

"I'm good at math." June said. "Maybe I can make it work."

"You don't even like this game!"

"I like that Jonny is making something, and it's well drawn, dude!"

"Good looks. I made it in lock-up, tried to play a game with Spider, he didn't get it though."

"The points problem isn't my only issue though. Masters of Mojo has a massive narrative! All the cards are characters from the lore, and Jonny Vulcain just does not exist in Apocalaya."

"Apocalaya?" June asked.

"The swampocalyptic city that MoM takes place in, keep up, June."

"I could exist in Apocalaya."

"Really? I'd love to hear how, honestly." Sherm reached into his backpack and hefted out a huge hardback book with an illustrated cover of magical bayou violence. He dropped it on the table with a thud, and stared Jonny down. "Read this, and report back. If you can justify to me a way that *you* fit into this storyworld, and if June can balance the numbers, I'll let you play your cards."

Jonny looked at June, and she nodded in accord. Together they accepted the quest as he spoke the words "Aight, bet."

# FOUr

"So I'll be back to scoop you in like twenty-five." June said as she strapped the large package of cannabis to the back of her bike. "That's enough time?"

"Plenty."

"Okay. See you in a few, hope it goes well."

"Good looks, me too."

In a thunder crack of exhaust pipes, June dashed off uptown.

Jonny retrieved the spliff he had stashed in his bike helmet and ignited it. As he stood and rallied himself, the chirps of a magpie turned his head to the tree in front of him. A black and white bird stared down, to whom Jonny exhaled a smokey breath of laughter, and offered a salute. "Wondered if you'd show up."

The magpie squawked.

"What's the deal, you scope out the situation?"

It squawked twice.

"Mm." Jonny sat on the bench under the tree. "This is stressful, bro." He looked to the magpie's reflection in a window above, and saw the bird stiffen, then crack like trodden charcoal. Blue flames roared from the broken bird's core, consuming the creature in an anime-flavour fireball. Feathers melted like plastic and dripped down burning. Jonny flung himself from the splash-zone, turned to face the action, but the bird was gone. Sat on the bench beneath was Charlie, spikey haired and ghostly, still eighteen.

"What the fuck, man?" Jonny patted himself down, regaining composure as he made certain that he wasn't on fire.

"You like that one? I've been workin' on it."

"I know you think I'm not fazed by this whole ghost thing, but bro, you just burst into flame."

"Pretty cool, right?"

"Yea, actually. But gimme some distance next time, damn." Jonny took a seat next to Charlie.

"You wasn't in danger, fool. It's just a game I'm playin' with the light. I'm gettin' pretty good at this spectre gig, but crossing over into physicality, not so much."

"Word. What you been gettin' into?"

"Just runnin' the regular dead errands. *Derrands*. Some guardian angel type plays, refining in the spook show, but recently I've been puttin' a good amount of time into just tryna pick stuff up."

"Pick stuff up?"

"Yea, findin' things I can interact with, so far I've got seven."

"What are they?"

"Mainly trinkets, but I'm stoked, I just found a pen! I've had a notebook for ages and it was frustratin' as hell, holdin' paper in my hands but having nothing to write with."

"That's tight man."

"The spliff we smoked too, that was a good one."

"True." Jonny hit his joint and held it out to Charlie. "Let's see if we two for two."

Charlie reached to take it, but once Jonny let go, the spliff hit the sidewalk. "Ugh, can't all be winners."

"Too bad." Jonny brushed it off, held the filter to a flame, and breathed life back into the cherry.

"You gotta get goin' anyway, fool."

"Yup. It's gonna go okay, right? Like, your pops ain't there, is he?"

"Na, he's at the dry cleaners. It's gonna be fine, Avir will be happy to see you, probably."

"Real vote of confidence."

"What's the worst that can happen?"

"Avir knocks me the fuck out on arrival."

"Na, man. He's disciplined as shit. He'd never get physical with someone outside the ring, unless they started it."

"He'd jus' finish it, huh."

"Wouldn't put it past him."

"What about your uncle? He a scary dude, man."

"He doesn't know who you are, not by lookin' at you anyway."

"Mm, okay, well let's do this."

"Good man. Love you, Jonny, thanks for goin' through with this."

"Love you too. Catch ya soon, I hope." As Jonny walked off down the block he looked behind him. "Hey, not for nothing, appreciate you leavin' me alone with that tiger!" The bench was vacant. "Huh, another disappearin' act. Would'a thought you were Irish with these fuckin' exits, Charlie!"

From a distance, the wind carried a magpie's squawk.

Jonny turned a corner and reached the East Side Boxing Academy, stood outside was Charlie's uncle, stout, broad, and bald, eating seeds from a bag.

"Coach Shah?"

"Who's asking?" He turned to look at Jonny with knotted eyebrows.

"I was a friend of Charlie's, I was wonderin' if Avir's here?"

"Huh. Yeah, but he's training. He won't take a break til half-twelve."

"Word. D'you think I could jus' drop in and say hello? I don't really have time to wait thirty."

"What do you want to say to him?"

"Nothing in particular. Jus' passin by, haven't seen him in a few years."

"Alright, but I can't promise he'll take notice of you."

Jonny followed Coach Shah through the gym; the air was wet, and smelt stale. Skipping ropes whipped the ground and gloves hit bags in violent polyrhythm. They walked to the furthest corner of the space, past the vacant ring, and approached Avir. He faced away from them, rattling the devil out of a speedbag. He alternated fists, bobbed and weaved, then switched foot position in regimented sets. His upper body moved as a unit, disarmingly swift, anchored and steadfast. He didn't acknowledge their arrival.

Coach Shah looked at the large clock beside the ring. "Give him half a minute. I'll leave you two to it."

Avir saw the second hand hit twelve and turned around. "Hi, Jonny."

"Hey, man."

Avir walked past him and grabbed a set of gloves. "You're not in prison."

"Na, got out 'bout a month ago."

"It's not a good time to talk."

"Word. You've not got five minutes real quick?"

"If you train with me." He slipped his gloves over well-wrapped iron hands.

"Yeah?"

"Tighten these."

Jonny pulled the velcro straps taut. "I'm down. What d'you need?"

"Hold the bag."

"Aight." Jonny stood behind the bag that Avir pointed to and braced himself against it.

When the looming second hand hit twelve, Avir unleashed hell on the punching bag. Jonny had half the wind knocked out of him and doubled the effort he was putting into stabilising the target.

"Why are you here?"

"I wanted to see that you're doing okay."

"I am doing okay, I miss Charvik, but other things are good."

"That's good. Are you still competin'?"

"No." Avir hit the bag with a straight right hand that lost Jonny his footing.

"How come?"

"I lost my motivation, Charvik was what made it fun. The fights I had after he died just felt like training, but with added pressure. He used to tell me jokes when he gave me water between rounds."

Avir maintained speed and precision, while keeping his breath metered. "I realised I was never competing for myself when I won and couldn't hear him cheering."

"Word."

"My amateur record is twenty-eight-and-oh, Jonny. I'm happy with that. A lot of people doubted I was capable to compete at all, but I found my own way. Charvik showed me I can do anything I set my mind to."

"Charlie was great at bringin' out the best in people."

"He still is."


On the third rotation of the minute hand, Avir stopped.

"Water." Avir pointed to a squeezy bottle in his gym bag.

"Got you, champ."

"In movies, people fight in prison. Did you fight?"

"Na, man. Squared up a couple times, but never threw hands. My cellmate was an OG, so no one really messed with me."

"He was your friend?"

"More like a grandad, Spider, I owe him a lot. He taught me discipline and patience."

"Those are important things. Maybe if you learnt them sooner, Charvik would still be here."

Jonny hung his head.

"Are you sad?"

"Yea. That was pretty heavy."

"I'm sorry, but maybe it's true. My dad says it's your fault. I don't know though, if it was meant to be that Charvik died, and you went to prison, who are we to question or hold resentment? I forgive you, Jonny. You should forgive yourself."

"Thank you, Avir. I think that's gonna be a long road for me."

Coach Shah walked over to them holding a pair of gloves. "About time to spar, huh?"

"In forty seconds. But I think I want to keep training with Jonny."

Jonny's eyes widened.

"*Jonny*? Guess you forgot to mention your fucking name, huh! What the fuck are you doing here? You think I don't know what you did to my nephew?"

As Coach Shah advanced on Jonny with dilated pupils, Avir put out his arm to stop him. "It's okay, uncle. I'm glad Jonny's here. I think it shows a good deal of respect that he came to see me."

Coach Shah looked at Avir and calmed a touch. "I don't like it."

"Uncle."

"Okay, I trust you. If you're straight, then, do your thing." He looked at Jonny. "But don't you dare step a toe outta line, huh." He threw the gloves at Jonny's gut. "Put 'em on. I'll set the clock and leave you two to it."

"Dude, are we gettin' in the ring?"

"Yep, partner work for the next fifteen, ten minute cool down, then lunch."

Jonny pulled the straps tight with his teeth. "I kinda gotta get goin' in ten."

"That's fine, uncle will swap in."

"Okay, but don't we need mouth guards or summin'?"

"*I* don't, and you don't have one. Besides, we have more to speak about."

Jonny's heart rate was high. "I don't know if I'm comfortable with this, bro, I don't wanna hit you."

"Don't worry, you won't. But I recommend you stretch a little." Avir rolled his hulking shoulders and shrugged aggressively with grunting breaths. "This'll be fun, Jonny!"

"Fuck, okay." Jonny followed him to the ring and slid under the top rope.

"See those lights in each corner? I don't like sudden noises, so we use them instead of a bell, make sure you keep an eye out. When they flash the first time, that's three minutes on the clock."

"Copy." Jonny limbered up and loosened his neck. "You're sure about this?"

"Yep, I want you to really come for me, don't hold back. And remember to keep your hands up, that's important."

"Got'yu."

The lights sparked and Avir advanced, eyes locked on Jonny's chest. His fists were low, his legs primed and loaded atop his toes. "Try and tag me."

Jonny threw a left jab to the chest that didn't land. He followed up with a right hook that Avir slipped, and with his face open, Jonny caught a light touch to the cheek.

"Keep yourself covered."

Jonny reset himself and jabbed twice to the head, both attempts were ducked, and he received a marginally heavier touch to his ribs. Jonny strung together a longer combo of punches; Avir bobbed and weaved like a machine.

"What happened that night?"

Jonny dropped his guard and got tagged on the chin.

"Hands!"

"Av." Jonny wrestled with his breath. "This ain't the time for that." He regained some distance with a defensive left.

"I want to know your side." He continued to dodge as he closed in.

"It's not a–ugh, short story." Jonny said, battling to keep him at arms length, unable to land a shot.

"The police officer said you was driving, fast, and drunk." Bam! Strong left hook to Jonny's gut.

"Yea–arh. Can we talk after?"

"No." Avir pressed Jonny towards the corner. "They said you went to a party in Rockaway. That you stole Sherm's mom's car."

On the retreat, Jonny's fists moved frantically; Avir's hips and head darted with hydraulic precision.

"We borrowed it."

Avir eased up on the attack.

"But yea, we went to a party." Jonny wheezed while regaining a balanced footing.

"You was supposed to go to Mars in the morning."

"Yea."

"Why would you risk so much? You could have just taken the A train."

"We didn't mean to stay out late. Our plan was only to go to the beach."

Avir stayed an arms length away, bouncing on the balls of his feet, Jonny struggled to maintain steady breathing.

"But you *did*. I don't understand why."

"Why what?"

"Why you thought it was okay to be so careless with your lives—with Charvik's life."

Jonny threw a sloppy jab. Avir swatted it away and stung his open side.

"Ugh! We was stupid, we thought the world couldn't hurt us. We was wrong."

Avir kept his stare locked on Jonny's chest. "Your corner lost that night. You all suffered, and you made my family suffer."

"I know." Jonny panted for air. "I'm sorry. I will always be sorry."

"I don't want an apology." Avir tapped Jonny's chin. "Hands! I know you are sorry. I want to know why. The last time I saw you, you said goodbye to me. You said you were flying to The Red Planet and I would never see you again."

"Mm."

"So what possessed you to throw that away?"

"I don't know."

"You are smart, Jonny" Avir kept him moving with two quick punches to his guarded body. "And Charvik was smarter. But together you were stupid."

Jonny's vision was spinning. "I didn't—I couldn't..."

"Hands!" Avir clipped him harder.

"How?! How was I meant to leave?"

"Get an early night and get on your spaceship."

"It's, it's not that simple."

"You second-guessed a huge decision. A choice that *you* made. And it hurt everybody."

"I know."

"So you *do* know?"

"What?"

"You know why we are here, you know why *you* are here. And now *I* know, I know why Charvik is gone." Avir pressed forward and worked Jonny's torso.

"I'm sorry." He said with the shadow of his breath.

"Stop with sorry! There is no pity, there is nothing to forgive, there is only now! So stand with what you have done. Stand and fight!"

Jonny threw a flurry of flailing punches, and he roared. Violently, from the fiery mantle of his being, he yelled a primal scream that vibrated his skull.

Wincing at the sound, Avir dropped guard to cover his ears. Bam! Jonny clocked him on the chin. His skin rippled, but his head stood concrete. As he absorbed the blow, his eyes grew dark, and his stature broadened. All signs of friendship abandoned his face. Rising from beneath Avir's feet, through his legs, across his torso, and into his fist, a bolt of power cracked Jonny in the ribs. He was knocked against the ropes like a ragdoll, jellied legs sent him to the canvas. The lights in the corner of the ring flashed. Avir stood, hands behind his head, face contorting from the pain he had inflicted. "Uncle!"

Coach Shah was already in the ring, he propped Jonny up and checked his pupils. "You with me?"

"Huh."

"Jonny, I'm sorry! I–uh! You hit my face!"

"You told me too–uh, ah!" Jonny cringed at the sharpness of Coach Shah's hand under his shirt.

"I didn't think you could! Oh, Jonny, I'm so sorry!"

"Fractured rib. You'll live." Coach Shah slowly lifted Jonny to his feet.

"Ah, no! Jonny, I didn't mean to!"

"Fuck, it's alright, big man. Stop with sorry." Jonny held out his gloves for Coach Shah to remove. "Should I go to the emergency room, or something?"

"You have insurance?"

"No."

"There's your answer. Not much to do for a fractured rib, go home, rest."

"Okay, guess I'll shoot. Don't sweat it, Avir." Jonny held his side and grappled down from the ring. "You got twelve minutes of sparrin' left, keep those hands up, champ."

Avir faught against the woe that consumed him. "It was good to see you, Jonny. Thank you for coming."

"Thanks for havin' me. Beautiful place you got here, Coach."

"Ice it." Coach Shah said.

Jonny grimaced as he picked up his bike helmet.
"It'll bring the swelling down."

Jonny turned the corner and returned to June's drop-off point.
Loud pipes thundered down the ave and grew nearer.

"You look like shit. What happened?"
"I'll tell you at the crib. Ride slow, I'm tender."

They headed downtown and across the Williamsburg Bridge.
Jonny held his side and gripped the grab rail. They rode into
Brooklyn and rumbled along Broadway. Tunring onto Myrtle
Ave, June yelled something he didn't catch. Jonny prided himself
on being a great pillion passenger, but right now he felt like
dead weight, and figured she was scolding him for throwing
off her balance. His head was spinning, and his body rattled;
every bump in the road twisted the knife in his torso. Dizziness
crept over him as he gazed at the urban landscape passing by.
The busy parade of storefronts thinned out, interspersed with
residential buildings and empty lots. Waiting for the traffic light
on Evergreen, the weight of his eyelids became immeasurable,
he began to drift. Accelerating away, he jolted awake, and
steadied himself with June's shoulder.
"Dude!"
Jonny opened his mouth to apologise, but the words stuck in
his throat. He was caught in a gorgon's glare. There she was, a
shock of red hair and a villainous silhouette, stood outside the
front building of a small industrial yard in a pinstripe pencil
skirt-suit and haze of cigarette smoke. The building was old, but
the sign was new, it read 'Ormen Moving Co.'

# FiVE

"Officially moving forward to the All City Apocolaya finals, a big cheer please for Green Light Leisures reigning champion... Sherman Glassberg!"

"Sherm! Sherm! Sherm!" The hobby store erupted as Sherm lifted aloft a mighty broadsword embellished with glass emeralds and leather. He held it over his head and beamed.

The battle fought was long, the road to victory arduous. Countless Saturdays spent at the war table, infinite mornings spent at the painting station. Sherm was cemented as force to reckon with. Three consecutive years he had dominated the local competition, combining calculated strategy with pristinely painted miniatures. Standing in the glow of today's victory, the shadow of his next fight loomed large. Sherm was in position to take the New York City title, a battle he had never walked away from victorious.

"Congratulations, Sherm." The store owner said as he shook his hand. "You've come a great way, and you do Green Light proud."

"Thank you, Barney. It means a lot." Sherm held the sword with its point to the ground and reached into his back pocket.

"After every game, like clockwork!"

"Can I take Swampslayer?"

"You want to hold the sword while you smoke?"

"Yeah, kinda."

"Ha! Go on, enjoy your moment."

Sherm stood against the shop window, looking out on the street. He tapped his cigarette thrice upon the sword's hilt, lit, and inhaled. The sun beat and the street moved. Sherm stood atop a mountain.

"Sherm?"

He turned.

"I thought that was you! Hey!" Kate rested her headphones around her neck.

"What are you–hi! Erm, it's nice to–yeah."

"Yeah?"

"It's nice to see you! Hi."

"*You're* high. Cool sword."

"Thanks. I am. What are you doing in Greenpoint?"

"Ha, I was at the roller rink." She twirled to show the skates hanging from her shoulder.

"Cool, they match your hair."

"And you're here to kick ass and take names? The cigarette-smoking serpent-slaying swordsman?"

"Pretty much."

"How fuckin' cool do you think you look right now?"

"Pretty cool."

"Huh, for real though, what's good with the sword?"

"I was playing Masters of Mojo, city semi-finals, and this is the trophy for store champion."

"Okay, less cool."

"Er, more cool."

"Did you win?"

"Do you think they give swords to losers?"

"Um, alright. Good job! I never noticed this place before."

"Greatest game store you could hope to find."

"I'll make a note for Christmas, two kid brothers."

"Are you hungry?"

"Hungry?"

"Eat. Do you want to go and eat? I know the best diner in the area."

She slouched and lifted her gaze to the clouds.

Sherm's brow knitted.

"Sure!" Her posture popped back to present and perky. "I was gonna go to Odessa, but eating before the train works better." She bobble-head nodded.

"Sweet! I just need to pack up my models. You wanna wait out here?"

"Can I come in?"

"Um, sure."

Kate followed Sherm into the store, a few conversations dropped.

"Come to the back, my guyzers are over there."

"Your guyzers?"

"My little guyzers." Sherm lead her past several large tables of battle, terrestrialised with miniature buildings, land flocked and sand sprinkled.

"Great game, Sherm! You're the man." A teenager reached for Sherm's shoulder as he passed.

"Thanks, Willy."

The walls of the store bore a cardboard quilt of fantasy art. Garishly bright books and boxes lined the shelves, carefully arranged and curated. Spinning racks of stock sat amongst the remaining space.

"It's not usually this busy."

"It's... *cool.*"

"And here is my battle-true band of bandits."

"Your guyzers?"

"Yes, indeed."

"Cute! Can I see?"

"Sure, just pick it up from the base."

Kate picked up a wizard model, being delicate to only touch its thirty-two millimetre base. "This is awesome! You painted this?"

"Yup, that's Train-Hop Warlock, the magnificent mystical drifter."

"There's so much detail, dude! The stitching on his patch repairs, the glow from his walking-stick-thingy, he's even got tiny eyebrows under the hat! What?! Who would even see that?"

"You did, right then!" Sherm balanced the sword precariously, and pulled a plastic tub from under the table, half-filled with loose layers of packing foam.

"Sherm, Sherm, can we hold the sword while you pack up?" Two eager kids ran to his side.

"Er, yeah. That would be really helpful actually."

Both kids dropped to one knee, bowed their heads, and raised their hands. Sherm place the sword across their palms in theatrical fashion.

"Why thank you, young squires."

"Aww, they're adorable!" Her head lulled, then snapped to attention; she reached across the swampscape for another model. "Oo, who's this?"

"Ah, that's Dominique, the dungeon mistress of pain."

"I like her whip, and those boots. You really nailed the latex, it looks all oiled up!"

"Thanks, glazed in highlights and semi-gloss varnish." Sherm laid the models flat on each level of the foam stack.

"This one's just a goat."

"Oh, yeah. Tin-Can Billy, he's just a goat."

"Sweet."

Sherm carried his box of models down the ave to the diner.

"I can't believe you don't get to take the sword home!"

"Na, the store has to keep it up on display."

"That doesn't bug you?"

"I mean, it would be a shame for the sword to sit in my room, where no one could see it."

"*You* would see it. I bet you'd pose in front of the mirror with it too."

"What?"

"Yup, bedroom mirror, in the nude."

"No way."

"Oh my god, you would definitely do that film poster pose,

where you're stood like all straight and strong, holding the blade like this in front of your face." She mimed something similar to a stoic monk.

"I definitely do not want to pose naked in front of a mirror with my sword."

"What *would* you do if you had the sword then?"

"I don't know. I might be inclined to have my homie June snap some flicks of me wielding it."

"She's a photographer?"

"In her leisure time, portraits mainly."

"Like fantasy roleplay dress-up portraits?"

"More like intensely-sexual erotic portraits."

"Oh, *Sherm.*"

"No, wait–that made it sound like I wanna take nude sword photos."

"*Yes!* I *knew* you were freaky."

"Jheez, forget I said anything."

"No, I'd rather keep my mental image of the birthday-suit swordsman."

Sherm turned scarlet. "Erm, we're here. This is the spot."

"Let me–" Kate skipped two steps and swept the door open.

"Ah, thanks!" Sherm shimmied through with his tub of toys and lead them to a booth near the window. "Hey, Andrzej!" He called to the back counter over the jukebox buzz.

"Hello, Sherm! Be right with you."

"Wow, Mr. Popular round here."

"Ha, it's just my neighborhood. I've been coming to Diner America and Green Light Leisures since before I can remember."

"How are you doing, my friend? Welcome." Andrzej said as they sat down.

"Very well, thanks! How are you?"

"Same as ever, living the dream." He handed them both menus. "You want orange fizz?"

"Are you kidding, on a day like today? Absolutely. You should get one, Kate, freshly squeezed OJ with seltzer and ice."

"That sounds good, yea, I'll take one too, please."

"Two orange fizz, coming right up."

"Thank you."

"You know, a gripe I've always had with freshly squeezed, it's never cold. Like, it comes out orange temperature."

"That's silly, you can just refrigerate the juice." Kate perused the menu.

"Yeah, but clearly I'm talking about very freshly squeezed juice. Like the juice we have coming, it's not even juice yet, it currently still exists as oranges."

A machine clunked in the background.

"*Now* it's juice."

"Huh, I see your point. But tell me, besides the oranges, what's good here?"

"It's all good, pancakes, eggs, sandwiches. I'm going for a cheeseburger."

"Oo, nice." She flipped the menu back and forth.

"There we go. Do we know what we're eating?" Andrzej said as he returned with the drinks.

"The usual, please."

"But of course. And for you, ma'am?"

"The same, please. It comes with fries, right?"

"The cheeseburger comes with fries, yes, but Sherm has hashbrowns."

"Ah, well, fries please." She smiled at him. "And a side of onion rings."

"No problem, I'll have it for you shortly."

"Thanks." The two said in unison.

"Mm, that's nice. Refreshing."

"*Right*? So, rollerskates, huh?"

"Yes, she rollerskates. I compete in derby, actually."

"What's that, like racing?"

"Nope, it's a full-contact blood sport."

"You're kidding."

"Not really. It's two teams of aggressive girls, skating around a track, violently pitted against each other."

"You get hurt?"

"Oh, for sure. But you also wear the cutest outfits."

"This doesn't sound real."

"Would it sound more real if I said we use made up skate names, instead of our real names, and they call me Jelly Roll?"

"Jelly Roll?"

"That's me."

"Awesome, like Jelly Roll Morton."

"Like who?"

"Jelly Roll Morton, big music legend. He played piano in brothels as a kid, and then at some point, I think he like invented jazz."

"Woah."

"Yeah, you'll hear him referenced in a lot of songs, Grateful Dead, John Martyn, Nina Simone. A real *musician's* musician."

"Are you a musician?"

"No, just an enthusiast. But that's tight your name's Jelly Roll."

"Yea, I always thought it just meant coochie."

Sherm spluttered his orange fizz. "Jelly Roll means... coochie?"

"Ha! Yea, doofus."


"Can I–er, last night. I feel like it's weird we haven't mentioned the studio."

"Yea, that was really fucked up."

"I'm sorry."

"What? No, your boss is fucked up. I'm sorry you have to deal with that shit."

"Oh, that's how you feel?"

"Yea, of course."

"Thank you."

"Is he always such an ass?"

"Yeah, he flips out worse than that, sometimes. I mean, last night's episode was malicious, but at least he kept it verbal."

"He gets physical?"

"He's been known to trash the studio, break shit."

"He doesn't sound like a safe person to be around."

"Well, most of the time he's pretty mean and hard to understand, but he kind of manages his anger."

"Well that's not *so* bad." She said in jest.

"Hm, yeah, he's awful. I've never hated another human being this much actually."

"So why do you stick around?"

"I don't know, it's an opportunity. Like, I really want to get into the music industry, but I have no experience. I barely have an education, and I certainly don't have any connections. Small Hours gives me access to *something*. I've met a few really cool people from working there, but it feels like I'm on the bottom rung of a broken ladder. Whatever I do to try and move up, I'm still just the janitor."

"I would of thought you know at least one big shot label executive. I mean, isn't the whole music industry run by Jewish people?"

"No. That's actually a pretty harmful narrative."

"Oh."

Sherm stared into his drink and stirred. "Like, sure, there's a number of Jewish dudes high up at the major labels, but the idea of Jews running the media is super problematic. It's feeds into all kinds of conspiracies and racist tropes that are ultimately designed to dehumanize and vilify Jewish people. Also, we don't all know each other."

"Shit, I'm sorry. Didn't mean to offend you."

"Nah, I'm not offended, just calling out the stereotype. But if you'd said *the Jews* instead of Jewish people, that might of got my anti-semite-sense tingling."

"Well, thanks. Didn't see how it was hurtful."

"All good." Sherm chuckled abashedly. "I really just sounded like my mothers then."

"So what do you think it would take to get promoted at Small Hours?"

"Dressing the part doesn't work. Being impeccable at my job doesn't work. And bringing Jonny in only scored me half a brownie point."

"You don't have any other ideas?"

"I have one."

"Pray tell."

"So you know about The Bully?"

Kate smacked her lips. "Tuh, fuckyea!"

"Well he's the number one person Vinnie wants to come on the show."

"As a guest?! That would be insane."

"It would be television history."

"So you want to make that happen?"

"What better way to prove how capable I am."

"Okay. So what are the steps? No one knows who this guy is."

"Someone must know who he is. A masked vigilante like out of the comic books! Running around the city, beating up bad guys– *someone* must know him."

"Well good luck finding yourself a superhero."

"There's nothing to suggest he has superhuman powers."

"Er, if the stories are true, he's bullet proof."

"Pff, I don't believe that."

"Either way, I have no clue where you're gonna start with this."

"I have a start."

"Oh, go on."

"So I know this dude, Detective Patchouli, he's been obsessed with tracking down The Bully."

"You're workin' with a cop on this?"

"No, he's not really a detective, he just thinks he is."

"Um, so a delusional person?"

"That's an accurate description. But he's not crazy, he's just got a few screws loose. The work he's done on the case is pretty impressive, he's got a big map with all the locations thumb pinned with string, newspaper clippings on a corkboard."

"Sounds legit. How did you get involved with him?"

"Long story short, Jonny and I kinda knew him as kids, he was just one of those neighborhood characters that's always around and everyone half-knows. I don't see him for years, then two weeks ago I bump into him tripping sack on acid."

"He was trippin' or you were?"

"I was. He starts talking to me about The Bully, asking if I have any information that could help him in his search, I laugh it off. Couple days later, Jonny and I are smoking, and the spliffs start talking. See, Vinnie has a reward for whoever can connect him with The Bully, and so we think maybe it's worth asking Detective Patchouli a few questions of our own."

"This is ridiculous."

"It gets worse. We leave the crib, it's around two AM, and we're hunting for Patchouli. We skate around for like half an hour, and boom, we catch him arguing with a deli clerk."

"No way."

"Yup. When he comes out the store we kick up a conversation, casually bring up The Bully. He zeroed in on us, like a shark smelling blood in the water."

"Shit."

"He starts speaking in hushed tones, almost whispering, but he's filled with electricity. The more interest we show, the more excited he gets. Finally he tells us, buy him a pack of Newports and we can see what he's built against him so far. Naturally, we oblidge. So he takes us to his apartment, it's a fucking bombsite, lorded over by his three cats."

"Cute."

"No, it stinks. But anyway, he's really got a ton of info together. Details on all the reports that made the papers, and even a handful of events that haven't been officially linked, but that he says are connected. It's wild, we've been back once since then."

"Do you think he's close to crackin' the case?"

"Who fucking knows, probably not. But Jonny and I are enjoying the chase."

"You're fuckin' cool man, full of suprises."

"Ha, thanks! You're pretty–oh, thank you!"

Andrzej returned holding two towering cheeseburgers with sprawling sides and a caddy of various sauces. "For you my friends."

"Amazing, thanks."

"Fuck me, this is a lot of food." Kate said when he was out of earshot.

"Uh-huh, I'm fucking stoked."

"Help yourself to onion rings." She said as she placed two under the bun of her burger.

"Good looks." Sherm said, diving in.

"Good fries!"

"So you're really close with Jonny, huh?"

"As close as close can be, yeah, I'm so glad he's home."

"Where did he go?"

"Oh, well I don't think he'd mind me saying, he was locked up for the last three years."

"Three years! What the fuck did he do?"

"It's a long story."

"This is a big meal." Kate raised her brow.

Sherm covered his hashbrowns in both mayo and ketchup.

"I mean, if you don't mind..."

"I can tell you, if you want, but it's pretty heavy."

"I can deal with heavy."

Sherm took a weighted breath.

"There used to be three of us. Jonny, Charlie, and me." Blood flashed across Sherm's vision, he closed his eyes tight. "Charlie was my best friend since before I can remember. Jonny moved to the city when we were eight or nine, and from then on, it was always us three." Sherm opened his eyes but didn't look up from the plate. "That kind of changed when we got a bit older, see, Jonny went to a different high school. I wouldn't say we grew apart, not even nearly, but we saw him less. He was so focused on playing guitar and he started dating Ava in a serious way."

"What d–nevermind. Sorry, carry on."

"Jonny's home life isn't my story to tell, but it wasn't a good environment. He lost pretty much all contact with his parents at sixteen. I only say that, because maybe it makes him leaving make more sense." Glass shards stabbed Sherm in the shoulder, he winced. "Like I told you, Jonny was meant to go to The Red Planet with Ava and her family."

"Uh-huh."

"Her parents are both scientists at the top of their fields, and pretty out spoken communists. So I get it for them, with all the technology up there and that, but still, it just seems so *alien*.

Anyway, I'm getting off topic. Jonny's set to go to Mars, not long after high school." Sherm paused to take three bites of burger in quick succession. "His last night on Earth, we went to watch the sunset at Rockaway, Jonny, Charlie, and me." He continued before entirely eating the mouthful. "We planned to hang there for just an hour or so, then head back to June's, smoke a couple spliffs, and drop Jonny off at Ava's." BANG! Sherm slammed his fist on the table. "We was only meant to watch the waves a while."

"Sherm, I'm sorry for bringin' this up, you don't have to keep going."

"It's okay." He said with tears welling behind his glasses. "We bumped into some older dudes we vaguely knew from the beach, and they invited us to a house party. *Fuck*, we shouldn't of gone, but we did. We start drinking, we've already been smoking, and some guy gives us half an ecstacy pill each. We're fucking raging like there's no tomorrow." Tears made tracks down Sherm's round rose cheeks, and his voice quivered in the back of his throat. "I think we were all trying to ignore the fact that this was the last time we would all be together. It was around five when we left, we stole a box of pizza from the party in hopes of sobering up, and jumped in the car." Sherm shut his eyes. "Jonny said he was driving." The darkness made space for images of tragedy and he looked at the ceiling. Charlie's disembowelled body wouldn't leave his sight. "Charlie was–he always rode shotgun!" Sherm wept and Kate held his forearm. A bubbling mess, his following words were unintelligible.

They were doing ninety over Cross Bay Boulevard, the water stretched out either side and underneath the road. Music blasted from Sherm's mom's SUV. Charlie stuck his torso out the window, soaring, one hand anchoring him, the other riding the wind. Jonny pulled him in as they approached the Broad Channel toll, and they slowed to the forty mile speed limit as the bridge came to an end. Once the town thinned and they reached Jamaica Bay Wildlife Refuge, the road opened up again, and The Three Blunters let loose. Music up, full blast; gas down, full throttle. He took his eyes off the road to grab a slice of pizza from the back seat, he didn't see it coming.

Charlie did.

No possible combination of letters or punctuation would describe the way in which Charlie screamed. Pure fear emanated from every ember of his being.

The crash was not spectacular. The car didn't flip, or fly through the air, or catch on fire. The car crumpled. Where the engine was, just half a moment before, was now a telegphone pole. Blood coated shards of glass, and glass was everywhere, everywhere except the windows. The displaced dashboard decimated Charlie's body. Contorted and lacerated, he lay dead.

"I'm so sorry, dude. I shouldn't have pressed you about it."

"It's okay." Sherm said, wiping his face with a fistful of napkins. "*I'm* sorry, I'm a fucking mess."

"Don't. I can't even begin to–fuck, it's so rough."

"Yeah." Sherm picked at his food.

Kate felt hollow; harrowed by the story, hurt by Sherm's pain.

"I can talk to you about roller derby if you want?"

Sherm took Kate up on her offer and she explained the broader premise of roller derby, laid out the rules, and set a track-side scene for him. While Kate explained how she plays as a blocker, but would much rather play as a jammer, Sherm emerged from back out his shell. The pair laughed as they ate their burgers, onion rings, and respective forms of fried potato. Despite his best efforts, when the meal was over, they split the bill. She left for work, and Sherm headed home. He would have otherwise been horrified at his public hysterics, but optimistically, his mind was occupied with thoughts of Kate.

# SIX

"Are you fucking stupid?!" June shot at Jonny. "The combination of information you just told me makes *no* sense! First off, why did you not tell me yesterday you got threatened by Red Planet people? Was it supposed to be a secret?"

"Nah, it jus' didn't come up."

"You was waitin' for another machete-madman story? It would never have come up! Madre mía, if I ask how your day was, the question covers whether or not you were held at knife point!"

"I was *not* held at knife point."

"Whatever, he waved one around. I still don't understand how that leads you to this *big idea*."

"I saw M on the ride home, I know where they're based now."

"Right, M, who I've never heard of either."

"She's the herald."

"Sure. She's in charge of Mars mail. What good does it do you to know where she works? You want your money back?"

"No, I don't give a fuck 'bout the bread. But maybe I can find the letter."

"So you're a detective now? Hanging out with that cowboy crackhead has done a number on you. You think this *classified information* is something she'll just leave around for you to waltz in and find?"

"Look, Ava wouldn't say some shit she shouldn't unless she

57

really had to. If there's *a shot* at findin' the letter, I'ma take it. There's got'at least be a message from The Reds 'bout why it didn't fly—I need to know."

"What if it's all a lie, what if she's doesn't even have a stellafax machine and she's just a crook who took your money?"

"Ormen Movin' Company is the last herald left in the city, believe me, I've looked. She mos'definitely has a stellafax."

"Regardless, dude, don't get yourself killed over this! They sound like dangerous people."

"Or they bluffin' so I leave this shit alone."

"You *should* leave it alone!"

"And then what?! There's no other line of communication. This is *my partner* we're talkin'bout, my whole damn life!"

"Agh! I understand! But fuck, Jonny, you can't break into a criminal hideout and search for clues!"

"I know how it sounds."

"No, you clearly don't! If you did, you wouldn't suggest it."

"June—"

"No! You think you are action man, but look at you! You can hardly stand up straight, the whole ride home you're holding your side. I can see right now, when you breathe, it's hurting you!"

"Fine, my rib might be broken, it doesn't change things."

"I think yes, your rib *is* broken. Now if you don't see how that makes all of this ten times more ridiculous, eres jodidamente estúpido. You dog-brained boy!"

Jonny centered himself with a short outward breath. "It's on Myrtle and Evergreen, that's like half a mile away. I'd be crazy if I didn't go scope it out."

June pushed past him to the sofa and gathered ingredients for a spliff. "I'm done."

Jonny withdrew and sat at the kitchen table, wearing an expression of concentrated calculation, he continued scheming quietly. "She's jus' *so* local. Like, on our freakin' doorstep." He snapped up and looked at June. "Oh shit, that's probably how she knows *you*."

June turned slowly and her eyes pierced Jonny. She held him

with a razor-sharp stare and spoke gravely. "What do you mean, she *knows* me?"

"Fuck." A bead of sweat ran down from his brow. "Um, well, when I first met her, she said she knows who you are. She mentioned your business, and er, said that me knowin' you makes her suspicious of me."

"And you don't think to tell me *this*?"

"I er—sorry. It didn't seem like the craziest thing at the time, I mean she knew my prison history and everything, even mentioned some shit about my psyche test."

"Okay, so she has access to police files, but the police don't know who I am, not on record anyway. So how does *she* know?"

"Word, I did think it was weird. But now, like, of course she knows who you are. There is not a single person involved in crime, livin' or workin' in Bushwick, who doesn't know who you are. You're the fuckin' Queenpin. M probably smokes your weed."

"I don't like this, Jonny." She returned to rolling a spliff. "Not any part of it."

"Yea, I don't like it either, but what can I do?"

"You can take a long bath, and rest your broken body."

"Mm."

"I'm serious. I'm heading back out once I roll this, you got the apartment to yourself, put a porno on the TV and jack-off or some shit."

"Huh, I was boutta go to the woodshed."

"Okay, close enough."


June's pipes roared across the parkways as the city shrank behind her and she ventured east. The gas tank glittered pinstripe purple and the wind slapped against her matching helmet. The road rattled in tandem with thoughts of Jonny. She was either upset with how little he considered her feelings, or with how oblivious he was to her actually *having* feelings; she was unsure how much credit to give him. The lack of acknowledgement for his LSD freak-out a fortnight ago was irking. It was far from the first time that he'd run off without explanation on a dawn-breaking escapade, but it was the first time since returning home. The night that he got locked up, she waited on him from dusk till mid-morning, and that concluded with a heartbreaking jailhouse phone call. So after only three weeks of freedom, Jonny cycling erratically into the night enthralled by the fresh experience of an amnestic ego-death, June was left more than slightly unsettled. She was sure he'd spoken about it with Sherm. He always took great care to account for the Germ's glass heart; but from where she stood, Jonny saw June as made of stone.

Fuck it. The road was open, the sun was high, and June was on her way to visit Abuela. She went the long route, detouring vaguely north to entirely avoid JFK, and then cutting abruptly south to the coast. Meadowbrook Parkway was a beautiful road once you reached Fighting Island. From there onwards it was lined with wild trees, dense shrubbery, and quaint lampposts, with notable exceptions where the road abandoned land to bridge between boondock isles. Crossing the final estuary and widest reach of water yet, the road became Ocean Parkway and ran the fifteen mile length of Jones Beach Island. She couldn't see the shore from the road, but she could feel the sea beside her. Rolling waves harmonised with exhaust pipes, and the wet breath of her breeze pushed against June's leather. Breaks in the treeline gave sight to open ocean and brought with it a deep feeling of relief, of surrender. Comforted and consumed, crashing cycles of surf curled up in chaos.

The journey took June an hour-twenty. She pulled up, removed her helmet, and proceeded to turn on the slim spliff she rolled earlier. She peeled off her black biker jacket and laid it over the saddle. Her shoulders glistened with sweat and reflected the hot spring sun that beat down. Cool air from the Atlantic brushed her bare arms and she closed her eyes to enjoy the moment of respite.

She was back on Long Island around the corner from Babylon Cove Retirement Homes. When the spliff was done she donned her armour, mounted her steed, and headed to the community entrance a block away. She waved at the security guard and the gate was raised. There stood a few dozen single-floor houses in the complex, a central green common, and a paddling of ducks that roamed freely between picturesque ponds. She pulled into Abuela's drive and the door opened before she had a chance to ring the bell.

"¡Hola, Abuela!"

"¡Bebécita!" Abuela beamed so bright she glowed.

She reached her arms wide around June and June bent down to softly hold her grandmother's hunched back. The smell of hairspray was, as ever, an overproof eau de nostalgia.

"Come in, come in, it's too hot outside. I don't know how you wear a big coat like that on a day like today."

"Tengo que."

"You should be driving a car, mija, a big safe one, with air-con!"

"Estoy buscando."

"Good!" Abuela waddled into the kitchen. "Concetta's here, we ordered from Bang Bang."

"Okay, I'm not that hungry though."

"Of course you are. What can I get you to drink? Ginger ale?"

"Sure, gracias." When June had completed the process of removing her boots, she followed through the doorway. "¡Hola, Concetta!"

Abuela's partner stood up from the Chinese takeout feast that lay sprawling across the table. "Bambina, it's so nice to see you!" Concetta hugged June and they kissed cheeks in European fashion. She was dressed similarly to Abuela; they both wore light knit cardigans that hung down to their knees with satin blouses, and polyester pants. Concetta was the younger of the pair, but her hair was bright white while Abuela's was dyed an obstinate black. Both of them had beautifully sun-worn skin, and wrinkle patterns formed from decades of smiles. Abuela's eyes were lined with dark pencil and spider-leg lashes.

"June said she's buying a car."

"Oh, that would be great!"

"I think I'd prefer a van, honestly." June washed her hands and sat down with a tall glass of water.

"A van? Ay, mija, there's always something crazy with you." Abuela placed down the diet ginger ale.

"I think a van would be nice." Concetta said. "We can go on an adventure!"

"If it's got those soft comfy seats, we can. Hm, where will you take us?"

"Ha, where do you want to go?"

"How about Miami?" Abuela clapped her hands and held them to her chest. "I haven't been down there since I was a little older than you."

"Miami? I was thinking more like Jones Beach!"

"Ay, think bigger, Concetta! We already go to Jones Beach once a week."

"Yes, but we have to go with all the other ancient people, wouldn't it be nice to go just the three of us?"

"It would. Okay, make sure you get a good one, June, and we'll need a sturdy box."

"A box?"

"Yes, a box. You think we can just jump in a van with these knees?"

"Okay, noted, I'll see what I can find."

"Good." She laughed. "Now, let's eat. Tell me if you want anything heated up."

A suburban city of Chinese tuck boxes sat in front of June, her brain raced behind raised brows and bug eyes. She portioned some white rice on a paper plate and looked to Abuela. "Which ones don't have meat?"

"This one is tungfu, I think, there's egg drop soup there, and then these noodles."

"Tofu?"

"Yes, the tufu."

"Cool. Egg drop has chicken in it, though."

"Oh, I don't know, we didn't have these fussy eating things when I was young. We were just happy to have food!"

"Vegetarian isn't fussy, Abuela. But I *am* happy, thanks for the food."

"You're welcome, mija."

June chop-sticked a small amount of sticky-sweet tofu from the box, careful to avoid excessive sauce, and pinched a droop of the chunky noodles.

"These are hot." June said, confused.

"Oh good. Would you believe those ones came stone cold?"

"Yes, they're sesame noodles. They're meant to be cold."

"Oh, well I microwaved them. Is that okay?"

"It's fine." June picked tentatively at her modest portion.

"That's enough for you? Go on, take some more!"

"This is good, honestly, I'm not that hungry."

"Okay, I just want to make sure you're eating enough. You're so skinny, mija."

"I take care of myself, don't worry, Abuela."

"I know I shouldn't, but I can't help worrying. My little June Bug is all grown up, woman of the house now. I'm not there to look after you."

"It's been nearly three years and the house is still standing, so I must be doing something right, but I do miss living with you."

"I miss living together too, but I don't miss that apartment. You should see it, Concetta, no windows, no AC, and so noisy!"

"You lived there for forty years, Abuela!"

"Yes, and I never realized how much I needed sunlight till I left! I was becoming a little mole lady, pottering around underground."

"Well I'm glad you're happier here."

"Yes, it's wonderful. A real house, with open space, and my amazing Concetta." Abuela looked to Concetta and took her hand. "The best granddaughter anyone could ask for, to give me all this." She turned to June sincerely. "But you have to tell me if the cost gets too much, I would hate to trouble you."

"Stop that. I pay the same rent you paid in the sixties, business is great, it's no problem to put you up here. I'd do anything for you, just how you did everything for me."

"So sweet, bambina! You two warm my heart." Concetta looked on the verge of tears. "Now tell me, what's new with you? How is school?"

"School is okay. I have a lot to write, and very little time. I'm having a hard time focusing."

63

"Do you like what they are teaching you?"

"I like what I am writing about, but not so much what they teach. The syllabus is archaic, and honestly, some of my professors too."

"What d'you mean by that?"

"The reading they set doesn't speak to me. It's always the same five philosophers, and however *brilliant* they were, I refuse to center my work around the writing of women-haters and Nazi sympathizers. I spend hours trawling through footnotes to find the truly revolutionary femme writers that were erased from the conversation, and when I look for them in the libary, I have to wait weeks for the books to be ordered in. I shouldn't be single-handedly responsible for broadening representation in the classroom."

"You want them to teach about female philosophers?"

"Kinda, more specifically queer women, women of color, women who consider the contemporary effects of colonialism."

"You let the teachers know that's what you want?"

"Yea, but to them, we may as well be the quimera. Either they're scared of us, or they refuse to believe we exist!"

"Hm, I think what you're doing is very good." Abuela looked at June with a halcyon pride. "You remember the stories I tell you about my mother, about how she faught for the right to vote?"

"Of course."

"So remember, her fight didn't end with the amendment, she had to keep fighting another fifteen years! Women in the United States made a great change, but once they won the freedom for themselves, very few continued fighting for us Boricuas."

"Sure."

"Then you understand why the extra work *is* your responsibilty. Not because it is fair, but because the change won't come if you don't fight."

Concetta nodded. "Your abuela is right, and I think it's more important than you even see. It's not just making *your* voice heard, it's setting the ground for those to come."

"Sí, one day they will teach the things that *you* wrote, and it will mean the whole world to a young woman in that class."

"That's a lot to live up to!"

"Well it won't be easy! But believe me, mija, it will be worth it. When your abuelo and I faught for gay rights, it felt like we were getting nowhere, for years. Now I look at you, and see how you don't hide for a second who you are, I know we spent our energy doing the right thing." Abuela's eyes teared up. "I wish *he* could see you, he would be so proud."

June stood outside and smoked a cigarette. Abuela voiced her disappointment that she had started again, but stepping away for a moment to think felt more important than hiding the habit. She needed to meditate on the greasy takeout sitting in her stomach. She stared out in dazed dissociation and weighed up intrusive urges against their logistics. She didn't like the plan that formulated, but it did bring on a guilty buzz of excitement, and it alleviated the uncomfortable awareness of Bang Bang orange sauce in her system.

Taking a seat at the table again, June piled her plate high with all the vegetarian options available, and cracked open another ginger ale.

"Ah, you found your appetite! I'm glad."

Abuela asked her how Jonny was doing, how the cat was keeping, and if there were any updates in her dating life. June heard all the latest gossip from the retirement community, was subjected to a rant about lousy card players, and updated on the list of prescribed medications that Abuela was growing ever skeptical of.

After eating, June excused herself, and left the tap running in the bathroom for some time. She smoked another cigarette outfront, and returned to the kitchen to say her goodbyes.

"Are you sure I can't give you something to take home?" Abuela looked in the pantry for anything that June might like.

"No, I'm fine, thank you. It was so nice to see you both!"

"We loved seeing you, dear! I hope you get your essay done in good time."

"Sí. Say hello to Ceija, send my love to Jonny, and give Mika a treat from me! I love you very much bebécita."

"I love you, Abuela, I will. And thanks Concetta, I hope so too."

### Twenty-One Months Earlier.

June left Abuela's birthday soirée and rocketed through West Babylon. Since recieving a call from an old flame with kinks akin to her own, June was eager to return to Brookyn and ignite an encounter. Preoccupied with lustful thoughts of the coming hours, June raced recklessly across the suburban streets, and within two minutes of departing failed to see a large looming pothole. She klunked over the jagged hollow in the road and wrestled to stay on two wheels. Regaining balance June checked in with herself and slowed to a sensible speed. She aimed for the shortest journey possible and headed for the Northport Expressway. Not a quarter mile down the tree-lined road, thick clouds of steam bellowed from her engine. Engulfed in the fog of her careless riding she had no choice but to pull over onto the hard shoulder. Stepping away from the bike June cursed herself. It was approaching eleven o'clock, the roads were empty, and she found herself without a single bar of cell service. Weighing up her options, June turned on a cigarette. When it was done, and not a single car had passed by, she decided to walk back into town.

The woodland rustled in darkness either side of her, the road was lit seldom by the moon. Her footsteps turned over unsettling thoughts as she considered the type of people who might still be roaming the streets in a neighborhood like this. She was a few miles from Abuela's quaint side of Babylon, but a whole world away. She expected to feel safer off the sticksville country road, but reaching the flickering street lights of the intersection, she instead felt exposed. Every few feet she checked over her shoulder, her hand gripping tight on the flick knife in her pocket. She hoped a local business would still be open, or maybe she'd find someone walking their dog. All she needed was access to a landline, she had the number of a Brooklyn-based tow truck, and enough cash to entice them out of the city. Arriving at the edge of town, she peered into each window she passed. No signs of life from the illuminated interiors of Burger King, Wendy's, or IHOP. The uncanny series of mattress stores and car showrooms were all lifeless. The strip mall was dead; the gas station a bust.

"Fuck!"

No one heard her yell.

The surrounding silence was deafening. Undeniably spooked by the ghostly nature of the Babylon's outskirts after dark, June doubled back to where her bike rest. By the time she returned, nearly an hour had passed since pulling over; she hadn't seen a soul. Resigned to stress-smoking Marlboros, June considered walking her bike back to Abuela's. The trek would be exhausting and take at least another hour, but her main concern was that forever after Abuela would worry for June to ride her bike anywhere. Burning another bone to the nub, she was down to three cigarettes. Anxiety intensified.

At the precipice of despair, a stomping sound grew swiftly in the distance. June turned to see but the shadows showed nothing. As it drew nearer she recognised the rapid clacking as animal hooves striking asphalt. A single light cut through the darkness and was approaching at speed. June stepped out into the road and squinted to see what was coming. The light was without a doubt attached to the galloping, but what carried the lamp was no clearer to behold. Unsure of whether her situation was improving, or falling into a Lovecraftian nightmare, she stood her ground but stood still. The cantering light was soon upon her, and as its silhouette came into focus, June was met by a pony. The young horse was pulling a barebones metal buggy, consisting of an aluminum pipe frame, two skinny wheels, and a single seat that sat low to the ground. The pony slowed and stopped in front of June. A shadowed figure climbed out of the contraption.

"Bike trouble, hun?" Asked the midnight rider as she walked

into the lamplight.

"Yea, I hit a pothole and it started steaming." June loosened her grip around the blade in her pocket. "I don't know, but something is fucked."

"Mind if I take a look?"

"Please." June lit another cigarette.

The woman crouched down and inspected the engine. "You've got a crack in the radiator, doll. Big one."

"Great." June took a long drag. "Do you have a phone I could use?"

"No, don't have a phone." She stood up and wipped her palms on her jeans.

"Okay. I need to call to a tow truck."

"At this hour? Good luck."

June wasn't in the mood to recieve sarcasm from a stranger, but the woman spoke with a British accent, which for some reason entirely undercut the passive acrimony.

"Where ya gettin' back to?" She asked.

"Brooklyn."

"Shit! You'll be out here all night." She looked at June undecidedly. "Can I bum a smoke?"

June elicited a skeptical sound of woe, but reached for her pack. "Sure." She passed the woman her penultimate cigarette.

"Cheers." She took it and placed it behind her ear. "Tell ya what, come back with me, and my brother'll take a look. He can weld it up good enough to get ya back to Brooklyn."

"Really?"

"Yea, we're only ten minutes down the way."

"How would we get there?"

"Tie the bike to the trap, I'll pull ya."

"The horse is cool with that?"

The woman looked at the Welsh Cob. "Kushti, grasni?"

The pony snorted.

"She's cool."

"Alright! She's beautiful, by the way."

"She is." The woman reached into a small saddle bag and retrieved a length of rope. "It's a little short, but it'll have to do."

"You jus' carry rope around with you?"

"In case I fancied hitchin' the horse. Never know when you'll need to pull over and pee."

"Good point. Can I say hello?"

"Yea, she loves people." The woman turned to tie the rope arround the trap. "Molly."

June smiled as she stroked the firm cheek of the pony. "June."

The woman doubled over the frame laughing. "No, love! The pony's Molly." She looked up, composed herself, and extended a work-hardened hand. "Ceija."

June followed suit with freshly manicured nails. "A pleasure."

Ceija instructed June on the best practice for being towed, and they set off at steady pace. It wasn't long before they reached their destination. Down the end of a quiet suburban side street, a wooden garage marked 'Stallion Motors' sat at the entrance of a broad grass clearing. Behind the building stood a smattering of trailer homes, caravans, outdoor furniture, and automobiles in various states of repair. The space was open and well-loved, encircled by a dense treeline. At the center of the campsite, a knuckly mustachioed man watched the embers of a dying firepit. He stood as the pair pulled in.

"Alright, Thom?" Ceija called.

"Dordi, pen. You worried me! Av akai."

"Wait here, doll." Ceija climbed out the trap and walked over. "Where's Ambrose?" She asked when she was close enough to talk quietly.

"Passed out motto." He wrapped his long arms around her. "I hate to see you two fight, but you can't dash off like that this late."

"So I'm s'posed to stay put and let him bollock me? Leave it out, I had'a clear my head is all."

"But trottin' alone, Ceija, what if something happened?"

"Pfft, me beshav pe gadya buki."

"Misto." He looked passed Ceija's shoulder. "Who's the gauji?"

"A friend. Her bike broke down, cracked radiator. Would you mind fixin' it up real quick?"

"Right now? No, pen. Musai te sootti."

69

"Urgh, tehára ánde diminyátsa?"

"Sure, first thing."

"Her'y?"

"Hai'she'li. Set your friend up in the vardo." He hugged Ceija again. "Kushti ratle."

"Night, Thom. Love you."

Thom waved at June as he retired to his trailer.

"So that's a no?" June asked as Ceija walked back over.

"I'm sorry, hun, he's tired. But if you wanna stop over he can sort it in the mornin'."

"You mean stay the night?"

"Yea, it's no trouble, you'd have a lil' caravan all to ya'self."

June looked at her phone and saw she had cell service again. "Hm, if you really don't mind?"

"It'd be my pleasure." Ceija smiled and removed the yolk from her horse. "Lemme jus' put Molly in her stable. Take a seat by the fire, your bikes fine here."

"Cool, thank you."

As Ceija was about to walk away, she was arrested by a pressing thought. "Drink?"

"Oh, please. What are you thinkin'?"

"Beer?"

"Hm."

"Vodka?"

"Sure!"

"Lovely. Tonic?"

"Great. You're amazing."

June took a seat by the fire pit and watched the smoldering logs crackle. Ceija returned from the stables at the far end of the field and held up a 'one moment' finger symbol. She carefully opened the door to a trailer and crept inside. She emerged carrying two bottles, two glasses, and a pack of cigarettes balanced on a stack of freshly folded linen.

"Come with me." She said in a hushed tone as she passed by June. They walked over to a traditional wooden caravan, painted

70

with bright beautiful flowers and delicate patterns. "Get the door."

June unlatched the front and opened the doors to living quarters from another time. She stepped aside for Ceija to kick her shoes off and climb in. She placed down her bundle on the sideboard and switched on a camping lantern. Every inch of the interior was decorated with ornate detail, from the guilded ceiling to the antique carpet. Intricately carved skirting embellished all the fitted furniture, painted in bold colours with gold leaf accents.

"Wow."

"Not too shabby, huh?"

"This is incredible!"

"Thanks, Thom and I built it few years back."

"You made this?!"

"Couldn't exactly bring one from Britain." Ceija laughed. "It's funny the things you miss after a while."

"I've never seen anything like it."

"Well make ya'self at home, it's yours for the night, but shoes off mind."

June sat on the porch steps and removed her hulking boots. By the time she found her way inside, Ceija had made the bed at the rear of the vardo and was sat on a cushioned bench pouring generous drinks.

"It's so cozy!" June said taking a seat opposite.

"Glad you like it" Ceija smiled. "Here." She passed June a vodka tonic and raised her own. "To findin' friends in strange places."

"¡Salud!" Clink.

Ceija placed a porcelain ashtray on the step stool between them. She took the cigarette from behind her ear and swiped it back and forth between her lips before lighting it.

"It's okay to smoke in here?" June asked, reaching for her pack.

"S'long as you don't burn it down."

"Think I can manage that." June lit her last dart. "So what's the deal with this place, you live here with your brother?"

"Yep. Two brothers, their wives, the seven kids between 'em,

71

and my husband, Ambrose."

"Woah."

"Stopped here in ninety-five, so it's been what, six years? The boys built that auto repair shop in ninety-seven."

"Cool. You work as a mechanic?"

"Na, jus' the lads, I read tarot in town, work out the back room of some hippy-dippy crystal shop."

"Like fortune telling?"

"Basically, yea."

"No way! Wait, I think maybe you know my abuela."

"She lives in Babylon?"

"Yea, in the retirement community, Delphia Melendez."

"Shut the front door! I know Delphia, she comes in once a fortnight!"

"Crazy! She always tells me about the 'gypsy psychic' that she goes to see."

"Small world."

"She won't believe this. Actually, she will, she'll say it was meant to happen." June laughed. "But she can't know I was stranded on the side of the road, we'll have to come up with a cover story."

"Abuela means grandma, right?"

"Sí."

"Ah, amazin'. She's so sweet, such a kind heart."

"She's an angel. But now you know me, you call her Abuela."

"Really?"

"I insist, all my friends call her that, she loves it."

"Will do, doll. I have a request in that case too then."

"Tell me."

"I'm her *Romani* psychic, not gypsy."

"Oh, you're not a gypsy?"

"I am, but there's a lot of history with that word. Respectfully, we prefer non-gypsies don't say it."

"Gotchu, vocabulary updated." June smiled at Ceija. "But that's so interesting you tell fortunes."

"Eh, it's whatever. Decent payin' gig, and I'm my own boss, so can't complain. But no offence to Abuela, it's jus' a hustle."

"Damn, are admitin' to bein a con artist?"

"I mean..." Ceija took a long drag on her cigarette. "I know how to read the cards proper, I'm not makin' shit up, but it's like a theatrical horoscope. People come to me to hear about themselves, and I give a lil' performance that makes them feel closer to the cosmic."

"But it's a serious thing in your culture right?"

"Hm. People have this romantic idea of gypsies bein' all mystical, so it makes sense to play into that and earn a bit of cash, especially as a woman. But fortune tellin' ain't much more than a parlour trick to be honest."

"I can respect that." June nodded. "Abuela get's a real kick out of it so–" She tapped her nose.

"Appreciate it."

"A little disapointed you're not a real witch."

"Never said that." Ceija winked. "So what about you, what do you do for work?"

"Well, while we're being honest, I sell weed. Lots of weed."

"Really?!"

"If I told you numbers you would think I was lying."

"Dark horse, you. How'd ya get into that?"

"The short version is that my cousin knows how to grow it, really fucking well, and I understand buisness. Over half a decade in the game now."

"Wild. You enjoy it?"

"It's a lot. I like the money and the autonomy, but it's stressful. At least now I don't deal with the customers, any less than a pound and I don't touch it."

"So you've got workers doin' the small sales?"

"Sí, all over the city."

"Impressive."

"Thanks. I'm also in school, workin' on a degree in Philosophy."

"No kiddin'." Ceija stubbed out her cigarette. "Ya'know. I can't remember the las' time I smoked weed."

"No?"

"Na, some of Ambrose friends back in England smoked hash, but it always jus' gave me a headache, like radio static in me ears."

"I have some if you wanna try? I promise it's nothing like what you would've had before."

"I dunno. What if it makes me go all weird?"

June laughed. "I think you'll enjoy havin' jus' a lil' bit, but only if you want to."

Ceija looked at June. "You'll have some too?"

"Of course!"

"Alright, le's do it."

June clapped gleefully. "Yay! Can I steal some tobacco?"

"Oh yea, I brought these out to share." Ceija tossed the cigarette pack next to June.

"Thanks." June began breaking up bud in her palm. "So how come you left England?"

"Fancied a change. Me and Ambrose left when I was nineteen, my brothers followed us a year later."

"Mind if I ask how old you are now?"

"Thirty-four, and you?"

"Jus' turned twenty-two."

"That makes sense."

"What d'you mean?"

"You're make up is *incredible*, and you're out t'see ya grandma." June laughed. "This is a casual amount of make up!"

"Exactly my point, twenny-two."

"Tha's funny. But so you've been in the states a long time!"

"We have."

"And you said your brothers are both married with kids?"

"Mm-hm."

"Tha's nice, real family community you guys built."

"Yeah, it's good. I can't have children myself, so I'm glad we got their kids around."

"Ah, I'm sorry to hear."

"It's fine, I made my peace. To be entirely frank, I reckon I prefer the role of aunty."

"I get that. Now, can I tell you something about me?"

"Naturally."

June licked closed a lifted a perfectly twirlled spliff. "I am the fastest weed roller you ever fucking met."

"Too right! Shit, here we go I guess."

June held a flame to the tip. "You'll be good." She inhaled life to the cherry and passed it to Ceija. "It's strong stuff, like obnoxiously strong. Jus' take one toke I think."

Ceija pulled hard but prematurly spluttered a cloud of smoke. "Dordi!"

June cracked up with her. "Okay, one more. That doesn't count."

Ceija drew a lungful of smoke and exhaled in a vaudeville pucker. "Wow." She passed back the spilff and chuckled. "I feel like a fuckin' teenager."

"Is'a slumber party!"

"The American dream." Ceija topped up her glass with tonic. "So you got the lowdown on my home life, what 'boutchu? Close with the rest of ya family?"

"No, tha's it. Abuela and my cousin. My mom died when I was young. Don't keep in contact with my dad."

"Tha's rough. So d'you grow up with Abuela?"

"Sí, she took me in when I was nine. We never met before then."

"Really, how'd that work?"

"Well, she's my dad's mother, she hardly speaks to him either. When I lost mamá, I was taken to an orphanage in San Juan, Abuela found me there and brought me back to New York."

"My gosh, how'd she find ya if you didn't know her?"

"Tha's a story for another time." June finished her drink and poured another. "Actually, I have a little brother too."

"Yea? D'you forget 'bout him for a sec?"

June laughed. "No! Ha, I mean he's not technically my *brother*, but he is really."

"Circumstancially adopted?"

"Exactly. He moved to the city same year as me, same building. When his parents left, Abuela took him in as well."

"Tha's sweet, you still see much of him?"

"Not right now, he's locked up unfortunately."

"Rotten. How long's his stretch?"

"Seven."

"Bloody hell!"

"Yup. He's behaving himself though, should be home in three."

"Te del o del. It's not always an option to behave."

"True. But he wants to be on the next rocket to Mars, and I don't think he'll let anything get in the way of that."

"Mars?! Why'd he wanna go and live up there?"

"Love."

"Figures. Damn, she mus' be really summin'."

"D'you know what, she is! Ava, she's really cool."

"She's up there already then?"

"Yea, left last year. I miss having her roun', she has this amazing way of bringing out the best in people."

"Ah, like an upliftin' sort."

"Kind of, but also no. She's really friendly and loving, but she can be tough! Like, she pushes you to be better, calls you out on your bullshit. She's never satisfied with *good enough*."

"Oh."

"I don't know if I'm painting a great picture!" June laughed. "Okay, I'll give an example. I never liked school, I dropped out senior year. I figured why bother, buisness is great, I'm better at math than my teachers, and the other kids make me wanna claw my fucking skin off."

"Uh huh..."

"Sorry, anyway. There I am thinking everything is good, I've got my life on track, I'm *done* with school. But then I met Ava. She's *so* academic, top of every class, and she *loves* to read. She questions everything. To be real I found it annoying at first. We would be talking and she'd say 'oh, have you read so-and-so, they say blah-de-blah'. I *hated* it. It felt like she was tryna make me look uneducated."

"Still not paintin' her particularly pleasant."

"Jus' wait! One day she came aroun' unannouced, carrying a *big* stack of books. It was every single writer that she'd mentioned and I hadn't heard of."

"Wow."

"Yea. We hung out that day, just us two for the first time, and I told her how I felt. She was really upset to hear it. She said she saw me as the most intelligent kid she knows, so she expected me to be well-read. She realized already how different our access to education was, and that's why she came to lend me the books, but she never meant to make me feel bad."

"Tha's sweet, I guess."

"There's more! I got into reading those books and I fell in love! I always enjoyed thinking about *the big questions*, you know? But there was a whole world of critical thinking I'd been missing out on! She opened my eyes to studying for the sake of knowledge."

"Okay, I get it, she pushed you."

"Yea, and she kept pushing. We would talk about books for hours, and I even started recommending *her* things to read. She brought a passion out of me I didn't know existed, and she helped me nuture it! She convinced me to go back to school, and I was *so* resistant at first, until she actually tricked me into going to see an open day at NYU."

"She tricked you?"

"Sí, she asked me to take her clothes shopping!"

"Tha's fuckin' funny. So I guess you liked it there then?"

"I did, but it seemed so unattainable. I didn't think I would get accepted, or whatever other doubts I had, but she fucking *hounded* me to write that application essay. It's like, she doesn't jus' *wish* the best for people, she will actually sit someone down and make a real plan for how they can *achieve* the best."

"Wow, alright. Yea, that *is* a good friend." Ceija took a heavy breath with wide eyes and reached for a cigarette.

"You okay?"

"Yea, darlin'. I think the dope is creepin' up on me, my face is all warm an' droopy feelin'."

"Hm, I see it, your eyes are half way down your cheeks. Kinda like a Picasso painting."

"What?!"

"I'm kidding! You're still beautiful, but yes, you're stoned." June smiled. "Okay, I need to know, where can I pee?"

Ceija finished lighting her cigarette and lit up. "Oh! I need to pee too!" She exhaled and scrunched up her face in thought. "We have two options, creep into mine and risk wakin' Ambrose, or we pee outside."

"Outside."

"The ol' squat n'shake. Good choice."

Under a carpet of stars, they peed together. But soon they were both crying; for with their jeans around their knees, they were simultaneously struck by an insurmountable fit of the giggles.

## Present Day. May 17th, 2003.

June wanted to go home. She wanted to call it a day on being in the company of others. She wanted an empty apartment and an open road, she wanted to rewatch *The Hunger* on VHS and forget the world exists. She had, however, already told her friend she was coming.

She parked her bike outside Stallion Motors and entered the campsite. As she walked over to the stables at the far end of the field, she retrieved a camera from her inside jacket pocket and wound the film.

"There she is! How ya keepin', hun?" Ceija called.

"Wait! Hold what you're doing for a second." She snapped a series of portraits and smiled. "Hey! I'm good, thank you." She hugged Ceija. "The light is falling so pretty on you two right now."

"You're sweet, doll." Ceija removed Molly's bridle, hung it on the stable wall, and fed her a sugar cube.

The pair reconvened at the plastic patio furniture.

"So what's new w'you, love?"

"Mostly the same. School, work, living in a cave. Jonny's home, that's a change."

"Oh, wow! Happy to hear it, how's he doin'?"

"I don't know. Some days he is *good*, some days he is *reclusive*, some days he is *stupid*. He's put up walls, he's not a kid anymore."

"Hm, he had'a come of age in a place where tenderness is a weakness. He's readjustin'."

"He is, and me too, I got so used to living alone."

"I bet. Is he in the flat much?"

June thought about it. "He spends most of his day in the woodshed, he works nights, it could be worse."

"What's he doin' in the woodshed?"

78

"He says band practice."

"But it's not?"

"I don't know. I wanna not think about Jonny right now."

"Fair'nuff, hun."

"What about you? How's life?"

"Same old. Been nice today, little too hot, but had'a chance to read my book, take Molly for a quick run. Yeah."

"I was gonna say, it's quiet here! Where is everyone?"

"Ambrose took'em all to some water park."

"Nice. You didn't feel like going?"

"Nah, not much one for the water, me. Besides, been lookin' forward seein' m'girl!"

"Ah, me too."

Ceija looked over to the stables and her smile evanesced. "Can I tell ya somethin'?"

"Of course."

"Couple things been playin' on my mind for a while, it's—ah, you remember the night we met?"

"Yea."

"Well, the reason I was out that night, the reason I brought you back, I was rowin' with Ambrose. *Bad*."

"Okay."

"I needed'a blow off some steam, so I took Molly out for a trot, and you know the rest. But I don't reckon ya'd know what it meant for me to bring you back."

"It meant a lot for me too."

"No. Like, we don't *do* that. It's not a done thing to bring unknown gaujo into to the campsite."

"Oh."

"It was a dig at him. It was doin' summin' I shouldn't, cause I knew he'd hate it. Funny thing is, I never 'fessed up—made out like we was long time friends. It felt enough to jus' do summin' for me, like a lil' personal rebellion to remind myself I don't need to follow *every* rule."

"I never knew he was controlling like that."

"It's not all on him, it's our culture. Roma do things a certain way, lot'a beliefs n' traditions. Romanipen."

80

"Mm."

"It's why we left Britain. My gosh, June, we was proper punks! When me n' Ambrose was young, we had *enough*. We didn't wanna live like our parents, we put two fingers up to the old ways and decided to live *our* way."

"What didn't you agree with?"

"Agh, it'd be long to explain it all proper, but a big one was mókadi. Basically it's things that are 'unclean', it's more than that, but yeah. Both our families were well strict on it. There's rules bout everything, from what to do when ya blow ya nose, to what order you have to wash the dishes in."

"I never knew."

"How would ya?" Ceija lit a cigarette and June copied. "The shit that really got me though was the shit aimed at women. Genitals—"

June spluttered a cloud of smoke.

"Ya alright?"

"Yea, sorry. You caught me off gaurd. Genitals."

Ceija cracked a smile. "Effin' child, com'on! Yea, genitals—" Ceija cut herself short with a pained laugh. "Stop, you got *me* at it now! Anyway, *that* area, yeah, it's seen as unclean. Very unclean. In fact, women are dirty from the waist down."

"I see."

"Now, god forbid ya dare t'menstrate! Can't touch a girl if it's her time of the moon. Can't even call it a name, it's jus' *the thing*."

"Hm."

"That was the one that did it for me. The one rule that made me question every other rule."

"I hear you."

"Anyway, we left to start fresh. Take the things we loved bout bein' Roma, and leave what weren't no longer servin'."

"Sure."

"Thing is, as time's gone on, Ambrose ain't the rebel I remember. Sure, he don't care if I wash a pot before a plate, but the rules that give *men* power, well, he don't seem'a hav'a problem with *those* rules no more. Certain stuff crept in the last few years, he's upholdin' beliefs that he didn't have before."

"I'm sorry."

"I apriciate ya listenin', love." Ceija's presence shifted stonely pensive. "Now." She took a long drag on her cigarette. "I had'a tell ya all *that*, so you can make sense of *this*."

"Oh." June leaned closer.

"There's a Romani poem, *O Drôm si Baro*, the road is long. It's 'bout movin' somewhere new, 'bout puttin' strife behind ya, it's 'bout escapin'. The poem says however far we go, we'll know our destination when we reach it.

Kána aresas
Serel amên
O than katar tradilyam

When we arrive it reminds us of the place we left."

"Beautiful. So, like, the place you go reminds you of home? Because when you move, you bring home with you?"

"Kind'a, it's not so sweet. A lot of people got a problem with Roma. It's persecution 'bove all what made us nomadic. But the trouble is, whatever hate or violence we escape, we find it again. It's facin' the *same* prejudice that makes the new place familiar."

"Huh."

"But see, I was thinkin', I left Britain to be my own woman. I left to escape the traditions that kept me second. But after all this time, despite all my efforts, those things found me again. This place reminds me of where I left. What the long road represents, I feel it twice."

June sat with that. "Wow."

"I really felt summin' when I thought of that. I jus' wanted to share it with someone."

"I feel you."

"Thanks, love. Alright, I gotta start thinkin' bout gettin the dinner on. You fancy stayin' for supper?"

"I should head out, long ride home."

"No worries, before you go though, I got summin' to show ya." Ceija stood.

"Wait, I don't want to forget!" June ran to her saddle bag and returned with a crisply zeroxed zine. "This is a queer artist collective I know, they published some of my photographs."

"Oh." Ceija flicked through the first few pages. "Wow! *Okay.*"

June laughed. "Not your regular readin', huh?"

"Not by a mile. What photos are yours?"

June turned to a double spread of a ropebound sapphic scene. "All the pictures in this feature."

"Dordi! What kinda stuff d'you get up to? I mean, it's a lovely photo." She looked to June. "I can hold on to this?"

"It's yours!"

"Cheers, doll. I'll have a proper gander later."

"I hope you like it, there's some short stories I think you'll enjoy." June blushed.

"Lolilan."

"Sorry?"

"You blushed."

"I did? Funny, well I'm happy to give you a little window into *my* world." June looked away. "That's a pretty word, *lolilan.*"

"It is, now come let's hav'a look what Thom built." She started off towards towards the garage.

"He found a new side project?"

"Yeah, really got into this one, jus' finished it up. I put some work in an'all. Laid out a ton'a money on it though, he's pressed now'a sell it."

"Any takers?"

"Nah, Thom's bein' stubborn, says he won't sell to someone he don't trust."

"It's special, ay? C'mon, tell me what he built!"

Ceija cranked open the garage doors and June's jaw dropped.

"A van."

"You're fucking *kidding* me."

# Seven

The band kicked out the jams. Jonny shredded riffs and licks, Iselda laid down the bass, Altony obliterated the drum kit, and Lucky's fingers cantered across the keys. Space age sounds of the psychedelic met groove metal vibes at the Delta blues crossroads of Pythagorean time signatures. They sat in the pocket, they broke through the hem. Jonny was free, he danced with his psyche, and the elements existed in harmony. The band rose to crescendo, the tempo doubled; they charged and released. The last chord rang out, tape delay echoing from the rhodes, cymbals splashing to eternity, sub bass rumbling the structure of the woodshed.

Jonny clicked stop on the four-track cassette recorder. "Fuck yea." He sat down cross-legged and began billing a spliff. "I really dig that bassline you was hittin' with the octave, Iselda."

The pink skinned adonis sparked a long slim cigarette. "Mmm, that was a vibe."

"Mm, aggressive, especially with *you* accentin' the slap and pop with the kick and snare, Al. That shit was some sticky-icky staccato."

"Yeah." The round yellow greaseball grunted. "You an' Lucky found the space in it too, sat real nice in groove." He smiled under the shadow of his porkpie hat, engulfing the drumkit in an atmosphere of cigar smoke.

"Thanks! Ya'know, a kind word from you, Al, really means the world." Lucky's voice broke as he spoke from behind a wall of keyboards.

"Why you gotta go 'n' ruin it, ya blue fuck?" Altony grimaced and set his expression in concrete.

"What? I just mean–well, it's just that, we don't see eye to eye most of the time. It's refreshing–"

"I don't wanna see eye to eye! Matta'fact I'm glad that I hardly have to look at you at all with those new toys you're hidin' behind. You're a freak, a coward, and I'm ashamed to be associated with ya. If I compliment your playin', don't think it's a road to sharin' your emotions with me."

"Jesus, dude. That quickly?" Jonny winced and tightened. "Ten seconds, it took you *ten seconds* to sound off and kill the mood."

"I can't help that Lucky's lookin' for a bondin' moment when we're discussin' the jam."

"You can't help it, because you can't think. Like literally, do you ever vet a thought before it comes out of that axe wound you call a mouth?"

"Is that helpin', Iselda?"

"I don't need to think, I'm opperatin' on impulse! I'm a fuckin' man, and that's how we do. Gut instinct, baby." Altony slapped his belly twice in quick succession, producing audibly sweaty, unsettling claps. "An' ain't nothin' wrong with these lips right here. Believe me, the ladies love 'em."

"Gross." Iselda shuddered. "I'd swear you brush your teeth with a hand grenade, but I know you'd never put that much effort into oral hygiene."

"What the fuck are you talkin' about, Al? You ain't even a fuckin' man! You're an intrusive hallucination, a fuckin' schizo projection!"

"I don't think you're meant to say schizo anymore, Jonny. It's an offensive term."

"Who the fuck am I offendin', Lucky?! I'm sat in a woodshed talkin' to my goddamn *self!*"

"It's negative language, and you're using it to put yourself down." Iselda said. "I don't wanna side with mopey-bones over there, but you should be kinder with your self-talk."

"My *self-talk*?! You lot *are* my self-talk, and you're at each other's throats!"

Lucky held a hurt look on his face. "What's wrong about siding with me?"

"You're a scared little bitch with strangler's hands." Isleda shot back swiftly.

"That's exactly what I'm talkin' about!" Jonny knocked the innards out of his spliff in exasperation. "Shit. Look, I'm havin' a fuckin' hard time, I'm not doin' okay. My head is hectic, and it's not a fun place to be. The only solace I get is playin' music, maybe ridin' my bike, and occasionally in a game of cards. But the rest of my wakin' day, the sole thing I feel is chaos."

"Well, we are you, kid, and that's how *you're* feelin', so what d'you expect?"

"I don't fuckin' know, Al. Honestly, I still don't know what to make of you lot. Supposedly, you reflect me, yea? But I don't recognize myself in you! I'm not a misogynistic Italian warthog. I don't think I'm god's gift to the earth like you, Isleda. And I sure as shit ain't an anxious bastard who's scared of every little thing in life." Jonny looked at each of them in turn with their reading.

"So you're the only one with carte blanche to be a dick?" Iselda said, abandoning any humour in her tone.

"I'm sorry. This is just a lot, and I don't know if I get it."

"Maybe you're the sum of us." Lucky offered tentatively. "Maybe you don't recognize each us individually, but you can't deny the fact that you have impulsive tendencies, and–"

"And a suffocating level self-doubt that battles with a secret belief that you're one of the greatest living guitar players." Iselda finished.

"Eurgh." Jonny groaned. "I hate that that's kinda accurate. Maybe, I don't know. It still don't explain why Altony's Italian."

Altony chuckled. "Anyone who's lived in New York longer than a decade's at least a quarter I-talian."

"Is there something you wanna tell us though? You seem really on edge today, I know we bicker *everyday*, but I feel like you're a bit overwhelmed or something."

"Seriously? Of course I'm fuckin' overwhelmed! I don't know if I'm gonna be able to speak to Ava again, at least not until I get to Mars, and that's two years away. How am I meant to keep this relationship goin'? But more pressin', what the fuck was she tryna tell me that got red flagged?!" Jonny paused for a moment to rebuild the spliff. "The thought of movin' planets honestly scares the shit outta me, but it's the one thing I've been workin' towards. Now it's fallin' apart, and I can't do anything to fix it."

"You–" Lucky piped up but was cut short.

"And it's not even like I'm in a good place to deal with this drama. I'm fuckin' traumatized, and no one is cuttin' me slack for that. They threw the book at me, and locked my ass up. I'm talkin' forcibly ripped from my life, kidnapped by the state. Holdin' on to my humanity was an active fight for *three years*. Now I'm home, but where's my freedom? I have to structure my day around these make-believe band practice sessions, in a vain attempt to appease my institutionalized mindset, and it ain't workin'! Spider told me to not fear the voices. He said "Let them in, and learn from them." But what are you teachin' me? You're jus' holdin' a mirror to show how fucked up I am."

"Maybe that's the–" Lucky again failed to interject.

"The craziest thing though is you're the only 'people' I can talk to about this stuff. Sherm breaks down whenever I bring up the past, and June has her own battles to fight. I know how exhausted she is, and I feel guilty as fuck for bringin' her my baggage. I don't feel comfortable talkin' about my issues with either of 'em, and they're the only family I got around–ah!" Jonny's face contorted in pain as he gripped his side. "Plus now I'm gettin' visits from Charlie's ghost? That's weird. I'm not mad at it, but is it even real? Considerin' I recently made homies with a talkin' tiger, the jury's out on whether any part of my current experience is real. Either way, Charlie's only showin' up when it suits him. Fuck."

"Do you think–"

"I think of myself as this independent person, right? But that's jus' a lie! I don't pay rent, I don't pay for the weed I smoke, or most of the meals I eat. What kind of man moves like that? A fuckin' child! I can't even trust my own perception of reality."

"Have you–"

"I haven't had sex in over three years! I'm twenty-one, those numbers don't add up, it's fuckin' rage inducin'! Matta'fact, I'm officially declarin' myself a virgin again. Don't twist it, Ava is my *everything*, and I miss her for *all* that she is, every second of everyday, but wow, the celibacy is *killin'* me!"

"THA'S ENOUGH COCKSUCKER!" Altony roared down the rabbit hole. "I'm breakin' up this pity party. Sure, you got some shit goin' on, but goddammit get yourself a sidepiece if you're gonna cry over your lonely dry dick! If you don't like your situation, change it."

"KILL THAT NOISE, YOU SLEAZY GLUTTONOUS BASTARD!" Iselda ignited, her fuschia hair billowing flames of hellfire. "Jonny would never cheat on Ava, she is his person and their love is sacred! While they both live and breath, they belong to one another." Petrifying gorgon eyes sliced through the air and shrank Altony in his seat.

"A'right. Boundary set. No need to go biblical, I'm jus' tryna help the kid."

Iselda's nuclear reaction subsided, and she returned to a heavenly vision of sultry sophistication.

"Well that was... terrifying." Jonny said, jaw dropped and dumbfounded. He was frozen in awe until his eyes quickly closed and his hand shot to his side. "Shit, man!"

"Jonny, don't hate me for sayin' this, but you gotta stop pretendin' that you don't have a broken rib." Lucky said, looking incredibly concerned.

"I'm fine." He lied.

"Good stuff. That's bout the only thing you ain't complained about today, snowflake. Took your beatin' like a man."

"Ignoring an injury isn't smart, Al. If he's hurting, he should take it easy."

"Thanks, Luck, but I'm not gonna have a good time lyin' down. Relaxation ain't in the wheelhouse of easy right now."

"How about you playback a jam, lie down here, and focus on listening?"

"That's not a bad call, Jonny. Busy your mind, and take the weight off your ribcage." Iselda's tone was full of care, and it sold him on the idea.

"Aight, bet. I know which one I wanna hear, you remember that fourteen-four Aeolian groove we hit a few weeks back?"

"Sure." Lucky said.

Iselda batted her lashes. "How could I forget?"

Altony grunted through a cigar gripping smile.

Jonny rummaged through a Clarks shoebox of cassette tapes and pulled out a clear case with a hand drawn J-card. The cover read in bold graffiti bubble 'Woodshed #28'. He flipped open the lid and paused at what he found. The tape looking back at him was not one of the countless home recordings with a title written in permanent marker, it was printed with crisp black ink, and read 'Sorrow, Tears & Blood'.

"Fuck."

"What's wrong, Jonny?"

"This ain't the tape, it's Sherm's copy of that Fela Kuti joint."

"Would it be somewhere else?"

"Nope, I wouldn't have left that one loose. And I played my Fela tape a couple days ago, I know its in the case. Damn."

"So you think Sherm's got tape twenty-eight?"

"More than likely." Jonny lit the spliff he'd been holding between his fingers. "D'you think it'll playback for him?"

"What do you mean?"

"Like, when I play these tapes, I hear the whole band. But would someone else?" He looked behind him and studied the double-stack amplifier. The speaker cabs were wrapped in red leather, with purple fabric grill cloth, and the vacuum tubes protruding from the head illuminated the surrounding area with a Frankensteinian glow. "My amp ain't even real. I mean, I see it, I hear it, but I know damn well I'm plugged directly into the Tascam."

"So maybe that's what he'll hear. You playing guitar. No effects, no space, no us."

"Eurgh, that makes me uncomfortable."

"Wait, weren't you still plugging a mic into channel two when we recorded tape twenty-eight?"

"Yea! Oh, fuck, man. I need to get that tape back asap. If he hears me talkin' to myself like there's a room full'a people, he's gonna think I'm fuckin' crazy."

"You *are* crazy ya stiff-sock fuck!" Altony snapped. "All this analyzin' is makin' me fuckin' crazy too! I can't hear no more bout your mental health, jams from the past, or whether ya sadsack boyfriend thinks you're nuts. If ya wanna feel better, *do* something! Don't sit aroun' and wait for shit to happen to you."

"Don't listen to the meaty-beanbag." Iselda countered. "If talking is helping, we're here to unpack whatever's on your mind."

"Na, actually. I think he has a point." Jonny's cogs clicked into gear. "I have to do something."

"Like what?" Lucky said, audibly afraid to ask.

"I have to break into OMC."

"Tha's what I'm talkin' about!" Altony cheered and shot forward to grab the cymbal stand he had just knocked over. He missed, and it crashed loudly against the floor. "Whatever." He said, leaving it where it lay. "I like this idea. Show 'em you ain't no punk to be fucked with."

"It's ridiculous, you haven't thought this through." Isleda spoke as sternly as a school teacher. "What are you even hoping to achieve by doing that?"

"Well, obviously get the letter. Failing that, learn the reason the letter got flagged."

"And you're willing to risk your life for the possibility of *maybe* finding that? Why would they leave *that* information somewhere accessible to *you*?"

"They wouldn't. But they don't know that I know where their headquarters is at."

"It's not a secret lair, they have the name of the shell company plastered on the outside of the building!"

"I have a bad feeling about this." Lucky worried to himself.

"You always feel bad, Obi-Wan Jabroni. Look, I sneak in, I find the stellafax machine, and hopefully the letter's printed out somewhere close. If it's no dice on that, I'ma look for M's ledger."

"You think she just wrote this all down?"

"When I met with her before, she had *everything* written down. This notebook was *buldgin'* wit'info."

Iselda looked at him incredulously. "And you plan to get in the building *how* exactly?"

"Well I gotta scope it out to know that. But I got a couple thoughts."

"You're not a teenager sneaking onto a rooftop to smoke with your friends, this isn't playtime anymore. You might live outside the law, but you're not a career criminal. This is a step too far, Jonny."

"And these are scary people, they won't call the police if they catch you. They'll *kill* you."

"He can't live in fear of these commie bastards, he's gotta get what's his! I'm in full support of the mission."

"You're both full of foolishness! Firstly, Jonny's a communist, so that falls flat as an insult. But second, these people didn't move to Mars, they're here, making extortionate amounts of money off of people's need to communicate with their loved ones. They're aggressively capitalist!"

"What does that have to do with any of this?"

"I'm just sayin', Jonny, don't listen to Al. He's a sitting contradiction, none of his angry ramblings stand up to logic."

"Sure, but sometimes you have to take a risk for reasons that ain't logical."

"No, you *calculate* risk. It's literally an equation. What is there to gain, how much is there to lose, and what are your chances of succeeding."

"Okay, you wanna add that up?"

"My pleasure. The best case scenario is you find either Ava's letter or M's ledger then make it out undetected. The worst outcome is a violent death."

"Mm."

"Now, chances are, the letter's been destroyed. It's also possible M didn't write down the contents of the letter in plain terms. So, even if you *are* able to sneak in and sneak out, you have no guarantee of finding what you need."

"Fair."

"Weighing those hypothetical winnings against the very real chances of losing *everything*, you cannot argue to me that this childish endeavour adds up."

Jonny contemplated.

"I just think it's dangerous, you're nursing a broken bone, and–"

"Shut it, Luck!" Altony looked Jonny dead in the eye with a daredevil grin. "If you let them take this from you, where does it end? The world dealt you a tough hand, so rob the house, and flip the fuckin' table."

Sherm closed the apartment door with his backside, holding the box of models with both hands. He intended to put the breakdown behind him, and it was surprisingly easy to do. His therapist always emphasized shifting focus when he became overwhelmed. Generally, he put that energy into the miniature hobby, but today, he had Kate to think about. He left his tupperware treasure chest on the kitchen island and retired to his room.

Sitting on the fire escape, four floors up, water bubbled in a cloud as he ripped a mighty eye-watering bong hit. He wondered if she would come see him play at the All City game. He didn't want to get ahead of himself, but he felt on top of the world. In the same day he successfully defended the title of store champion, he crushed his fears of never seeing Kate again. They went out to eat together, and overall it seemed like she genuinely had a good time. He hoped she saw it as a date, but even if she didn't, they hung out, and they would hang out again, she said so.

Once sufficiently stoned, Sherm climbed back through the window, and hid his bong in the closet. He threw off his overly baggy polo shirt and cargo shorts, peeled off his socks, and threw them all in the laundry hamper. He grabbed a soft white towel and headed to the bathroom. He smiled in anticipation when his toes touched the fluffy floor matt. While the water warmed, he lit a scented candle and dialed in the seahorse suction-cup radio.

*The debut single from Evanescence is still topping the alternative charts this week. Taking the nation by storm with their first release, it's safe to say we can expect BIG things to follow from this band! Here is, Bring Me To Life.*

Sherm stepped into the shower as nu-metal blared from the lo-fi speaker. It wasn't his general taste in music, but he rarely found that on the wireless, and this song felt like something Kate would be into. He soaked his thick head of hair, and his tight curls relaxed down to his shoulders. Lathering himself up with a moisturising soap bar, he pictured Kate, and grew. He imagined her in the shower with him, the beads of water bouncing off her body. He wanted to pull her close and feel her breathe against his ear. He dreamed that the hands touching him were hers. Lost in fantasy, eyes closed and moaning gently, he failed to hear the apartment door open. He stroked and explored his pleasure, he teetered on the edge–

"Hey, Shermy, we're home!" His mother's voice cut through the moment. "You mind if I come in? I'm dying to pee!"

"Er–I mind!" Before he had the chance to answer, a hand gripped the bathroom door handle. "Just give me a minute!"

"Sorry, Sherm. I really gotta go!" His mom opened the door and sat down on the toilet.

"Mom!" Sherm was mortified. Bearing witness to the gorgon Medusa while in a compromising position, he shrank and froze, praying the translucent  shower curtain was opaque enough to conceal his shame.

"Eurgh, what is that you're listening to?" She said over a steady stream. "It's giving me an instant headache."

*Wake me up inside!* Blasted from the radio.

"What?! Can you go away, please!"

*I can't wake up!*

"Don't be such a baby, I've seen it all before."

*Save me!*

"Mom! Just let me shower in peace!"

"Alright, alright. I'm done now anyway." She flushed the toilet and washed her hands.

"Mom! Agh–fuck!"

"Sorry, did that get hot?"

"Yes! Please leave!"

"I'm going! I'm going!"

Sherm wrapped up his shower shortly after the interruption. He dried off, got dressed in his room, and glumly joined his parents in the kitchen.

"How did your game go, sweetie?"

"Good, I won."

"Great, well done! Now can you take your toys back to your room, please?"

"Sure, but they're not toys, they're miniature models."

"Yes, and they're very nice, but they don't live on the kitchen counter."

Sherm returned and grabbed a stool at the kitchen island. "How was the gallery?"

"It was fun, there were a few interesting pieces, although the bulk of the work was somewhat derivative."

"We had a nice time though, the museum has brilliant air conditioning. And we picked up a few bits from the farmers market on our way back."

"Cool."

"Have you eaten?"

"Yeah, I went to Diner America."

"Okay, well, will you be ready to eat again in thirty?"

"Sure, what are you making?"

"Stuffed peppers and latkes."

"Huh, I think I fulfilled my fried potato quota for the day."

His moms looked up from their prepping stations.

"That's not like you to say." She reached out the back of her hand to touch his forehead. "Are you feeling okay?"

"You're not coming down with something, are you?"

He dodged the temperature check. "I'm fine. I just don't wanna follow up hash browns with latkes, it'll put me straight to sleep."

"Suit yourself."

"Do you have any plans tonight?"

"I was thinking of heading over to Jonny's, but he hasn't replied to my message yet." Sherm flipped open his phone and clicked menu, right, messages; nothing new. "Hey?"

"Hm?" His moms kept their attention on chopping.

"You both went quiet when I mentioned Jonny."

"You told us not to say anything on the subject."

"No, I told you Jonny is my best friend, and you can't keep being mad at him."

"We're not mad–"

"We just don't think he's a good influence on you."

"Urgh! Still? C'mon, you have to let this go!"

"Let's not get into this, hun."

"But I'm not okay with it! It's so frustrating how you speak about him."

"That's why we should just move on from the conversation."

"It's not like we're telling you that you can't see him anymore."

"Well you banned him from coming around the apartment! You've made it *mighty* clear how you feel."

"Sure, we're entitled to our opinions."

"And we're allowed to enforce rules within our home."

"But we're not stopping you from hanging out at that drug den of a basement."

"Which a lot of other parents *would* have, considering everything that's happened."

"No! Stop, please. It's not a *drug den*, it's a regular apartment. And you *have* to stop blaming Jonny, it's not helpful for anyone."

"You always come home reeking of marijuana when you've been over there."

"And we're looking out for your best interest, he's bad news."

"*My* best interest! How do you know what *my* best interest is? You have no idea what Jonny's done for me."

"Can we please not do this right now?"

"No, maybe we should, Deborah." She turned to Sherm with a stern look. "Have you forgotten the hurt that he's caused you? How can you just ignore the shitstorm that he's brought into your life? Into all our lives!"

"Are you serious right now!?"

"Sarah, I just want a nice calm dinner together."

"You're in therapy every week, so I know you haven't forgotten."

"Sarah." Deborah said firmly.

"No, it has to be said. He's a convicted criminal, and he's the reason that Charlie's dead. That could have been you, Sherman! What if the *coroner* called us instead of the cops that night? You might think he's your friend, but he's dangerously irresponsible, and I do not like you hanging out with him!"

"You're so wrong about him."

"Look, I'm sorry, Sherm. *Your mother* is only trying to protect you, and although I don't think this is a conversation to have now, I have to say that I am on her side with this one. If you're going to move forward with your life, you have to have a serious think about who you surround yourself with."

"Why can't you trust me to make my own decisions? Jonny only ever looks out for me! He literally couldn't be a better friend." Tears welled up behind Sherm's glasses.

"He stole our car, got drunk, and crashed it! He killed your closest friend, and nearly killed you, so please enlighten me on how exactly he's a good person for you to spend all your time with!?"

The heat in the kitchen rose several degrees.

"It's not like that! You can't put all the blame on Jonny, I was there, every step of the way, and it was *my* idea to take your car that night!" Sherm stood up, emotion boiling over and breaking his voice.

"You can try and cover for him all you want, you won't convince us he's a sensible person. There's a reason he went to prison and not you! He's a danger to the people around him!"

"Both of you, please!" Deborah's efforts to calm the flames fell on deaf ears.

"You don't understand!" Sherm cried, his breathing firmly becoming hyperventilation.

"We understand just fine! But you're too young and too foolhardy to see it! We are your mothers, and we–"

"I WAS DRIVING!"

Sherm's panicked breathing resonated through the silence.

"It was *me*." He sobbed. "*I* took your car, *I* got drunk, and *I* killed Charlie."

"What, that–"

"Sherm, is this true?"

"When the police came, I was in shock. I couldn't–it all happened so fast."

"*You* were driving?"

"Yes! And Jonny took the blame, he told the police it was all his fault, to protect me. That's the reason I didn't go to prison, because Jonny didn't let that happen."

"Why didn't you tell us?"

"How could I!? All the horrible things you've said, how do you think that's made me feel? *I'm* the shitstorm."

"We didn't know, we–"

"No one knows! He told me to never tell another living soul. He wasn't looking for praise, he wasn't trying to be a martyr, but he sacrificed everything to save me."

"I'm sorry, I–"

"I need to get out of here." Sherm ran to his room.

Returning in haste with his skateboard in one hand and his walkman in the other, he flustered towards the front door, pushing past the arms his mothers, ignoring their pleas for him to stay. He blasted down the stairway, without looking back, and rifled through his pockets for a cigarette when he reached the street. He lit up, jumped on his board, and pushed away in a daze.

The evening air was sticky and gross. He wanted to crawl out of his skin. He let slip his most well-kept secret, and the thought of his crime being known by anyone other than Jonny made his stomach turn. The combination of quick movement and cigarette smoke made him sicker still. Three blocks from home he jumped off his board and threw up in a trash can. Disgusted passersby walked wide around him.

The violent expulsion of lunch was a sobering reset, the panic that flash-flooded his system subsided to a dull sense of horror, a residual dampness of self-loathing that he was accustomed to compartmentalising. He got water and napkins from the corner store, rinsed his hands over the gutter, and sat on a stoop to recoup. Slowly sipping the Poland Spring, he lit another booge, and untangled his headphones.

"Everytime, damn. How do they even get like this?"

Once he'd unpicked the elaborate knots the wires had danced themselves into, he reached again into his pocket and retrieved a cassette tape. He flipped open the case, expecting to find Fela Kuti's *Sorrow, Tears & Blood*, but instead he was holding a homemade tape marked 'Woodshed #28'.

"What the fuck?"

Sherm's confusion softened to a sly smile. He had pestered Jonny for weeks to sit in on a session, he had begged to hear something from his band, but Jonny wouldn't even tell him who he'd been playing with. Jonny scurried off to 'band practice' everyday and kept the rest a secret. Sherm guessed he'd been sneaking his bandmates through the side gate, but he never understood why they didn't hang out after the jam, or the reason behind Jonny's cloak and dagger antics. Turning the tape over in his hands he felt dirty, guilty for having access to this private recording. He thought about when his mothers read his middle school diary and put the cassette back in the case. Recalling the taste of betrayal, he decided to honour Jonny's boundaries, but burgeoning tingles of treachery were fueled by jealous curiosity.

"I mean, he did *give* me the tape."

Rationalising prying ears with the consideration that there was nothing else to listen to while he skated, Sherm slotted the tape into his Walkman, and clicked play.

# NinE

June drove her van back to the city with the radio booming and the AC on blast. In the dark leather armchair seat, she felt like a starcruiser capítan, the dash spanning the cockpit with illuminated buttons and controls. On her bike, June's default driving style was defensive, now she was damn near the biggest unit on the road. With the power of a V8 and the turning response of a maritime vessel, cars glided out of her lane when they saw her rumbling in the rearview. It was a mobile living room, an isulated bubble between June and the outside world. She could sing to her lungs capacity and occupy her mind with things other than her immediate safety. She could almost relax.

After a ten minute internal debate, she opened the windows and sparked a cigarette. The van had an inherited odour of stale tobacco, so until she had the opportunity to light some sage and wet wipe the interior, a little smoke didn't seem too egregious. Sitting in traffic through Jamaica, her eagerness to get home grew, but a thought crossed her mind that couldn't be passed by. She could buy groceries beyond her ten-block radius now. No longer was she bound by the local store selection, no longer was she limited to how many tote bags her arms could carry. Acting on the impulse, she double-parked outside the first halfway-healthy food shop. In a mad dash she grabbed an armful of ingredients, checked out, and dumped the takings in the passenger seat. She may have upset a few motorists with her hazardous occupation of Atlantic Ave, but that was an exercise in freedom, and she relished every second of it.

Getting close to Bushwick, she pictured in her mind an empty parking spot, focusing all her amateur bruja energies on manifesting a space large enough to dock the fifteen-foot vehicle. Cruising down Harman Street, she wasn't disappointed. Outside the apartment was a gap that posed no problem for the van. June lined up in parallel, cut the wheel, and reversed effortlessly alongside the curb. As she got out and checked her distances, someone stood from the shadows of upstair's stoop and clapped a round of applause.

"Wow! Fucking nailed it!"

June turned to see Sherm beaming back at her. "Ay! Gracias, amigo! Not bad for a first time van driver, huh?"

"Outstanding! Impeccable execution." Sherm opened the front patio gate and joined her for a hug on the sidewalk. "So, what the hell is *this*?"

"This, my friend, is The Vando."

"*Okay!* I want the tour, goddamn, you really found a crazy van."

"Ha, sí! But I like to think she found me. Ceija's brother built it, and he couldn't afford to keep it, so here we are. She's all mine!" June was giddy to share her excitement with Sherm, and he gawked at the van like a kid in a candy store. They walked around the machine's perimeter, taking in the sight. June told Sherm what she knew about traditional Romani caravans, and that Thom was inspired by a dream in which a shire horse gave birth to an eight cylinder engine. It was painted deep purple, accented with red wooden trim and turquoise panelling. It featured a fishbowl bubble for a view out the back, and a small metal chimney that protruded out the top. The roof was made of timber planks arced across its width, and they extended out past the end of the vehicle, creating a shelter above the rear double-doors. Intricate patterns were carved into the decorative wood frame, and the bodywork was embellished with pinstripe designs.

While sharing certain stylings with surf-wagon woodies, and West Coast lowriders, it was of its own volition, utterly unique.

"Wait, what's the thing it's based on called again?"

"A vardo."

"Vardo."

"But this is The *Vando*."

"Word, The Vando. Fuck yeah."

"You see this?"

"Ah, no way! That's awesome." Sherm crouched down to look at the chrome plated horseshoe that sat where a manufacturer's logo would otherwise reside.

"The best is yet to come. Our tour continues *inside*." June slid open the side door with a hefty pull, revealing a third armchair behind the passenger seat, parallel cushioned benches in the back, and–

"Is that a fucking oven!?"

"Kind of! Woodburnin' stove top, man. Cast iron kettle and pan, the works."

"Woah, that's wild." Sherm craned his neck to see the top of the stove's duct. "Oh, so that's what the chimney thing's about!"

"Sí, old school fume extraction."

"And hardwood floors! I can't believe this, June."

"Can you believe *this*?" June clicked a button beneath the third seat and swivelled it around. "They all do this, once we park up, it's like a fuckin' apartment."

"Insane."

"And you see those seats in the back? They both fold flat to make a queen size bed."

"Oh wow, fit for a queen, indeed! I'm so happy for you June, leather and everything, exactly what you asked the universe for. I mean, it's even purple!"

"It *is* purple." June looked at Sherm with the sweetest of smiles. "I'm so happy too, for all of us, it's time to start gettin' serious about makin' some cassette mixes! We gotta hit the road soon, hermano."

"Forreal. Oh, that reminds me, on the topic of cassette tapes–"

"Can it wait two seconds? I wanna get inside and start cooking."

"Sure."

June klunked closed the door and locked up.


"You were waiting outside, Jonny not home?" She asked walking through to the front room.

"Nah, he's not in the woodshed either, and he's not answering his phone."

"Madre mía. Fuck, I think I know where he is."

"Where?"

"Nevermind, I'll let him explain. Was you waiting on the stoop long?"

"Not really. I had a big blow out with my folks. Came here and no one was home, so I went to skate for an hour. Got back maybe twenty minutes ago."

"Cool. Not cool that you argued with your moms, just like *cool*, d'you know?"

"Yeah, nah, it's cool."

June started to prep sweet potatoes and preheated the oven. "Can you sort out the cat shit please?"

"What do you mean?"

"Scoop her poop and put food in the bowl."

"Aye aye, captain." Sherm went to the bathroom and dealt with the litter tray, only making a slight fuss about the smell. As he returned, the heavens rattled over Brooklyn, shaking the building in an Olympian clap of thunder.

"Hmph, I hate that." June shuddered.

"Fuck, it's boutta *pour* down! Glad you got home when you did. Where's the cat food?"

"That cupboard." June pointed with her knife.

As Sherm knelt down and opened the can of chicken chunks over the kitty bowl, tiny footsteps pattered towards him swiftly. "Hey Mika! Dinner's up."

"You don't like the storm either, huh, kit?" June winced as torrential rainfall exploded from the sky.

"It should pass soon." The second Sherm finished speaking, rapturous rolling cracks of lightning ran through the sky, and the sound of falling water intensified.

"Don't tempt mother nature, por favor."

"Word." Sherm chucked the can in the trash and jumped over the back of the sofa, landing gracefully in its cushioned gut.

"You hungry?"

"Yeah! Worked up quite the appetite, I don't know why, but I always skate best when I'm a little riled up. You should'a seen this shit I landed just now."

"What you do?"

Sherm snapped around to tell her. "So there's this thirteen-set behind some building in East Williamsburg. Spot of *mythical* proportions."

"What is a thirteen-set?"

"Ah, a set of stairs, with thirteen stairs, like a thirteen stair set."

"Jesus, okay."

"Yeah, it's high stakes, and the super kicks you out pretty quick. I know I only have a couple of tries to land something. I've done a five-o down the handrail before, so I ran that a couple times, but I don't know what possesed me tonight, I was fucking *determined* to kickflip in."

"Translate, please."

Sherm imitated the board movements with his hands. "So the board flips *that* way under my feet, then I land *on* the rail, and slide down it like *this*."

"You can't do that."

"You doubting Thomas!"

"No, I'm doubting you."

Sherm hissed. "Anyway, I throw myself down this thing a few times, land every which way but upright. Then boom, I catch the kickflip perfectly, and lock my truck in."

"You did it?"

"Wait. The super chooses *that* moment to open the door and yell at me. I tense up and land primo, hit the cement *hard*."

"Primo sounds good, no?"

"No, primo is bad. It's when you land on the board and it's sideways, like the wheels are adjacent to the floor."

"Oh, that's not good."

"No, I freaking tweaked my ankle. Anyway, the super looks at me on the ground, and I guess he was in a good mood, cause he says I got one more try, then I have to get the hell out of there."

"Nice of him, kind of."

"Right, I think he saw how much it meant to me."

"Sure, people don't repeatedly throw themselves down stairs for no reason."

"Exactly! So I get in position, and quiet every thought in my head." Sherm closed his eyes and readied his hands for a mime show. "I push off. Pop, thwick, catch, klink, skrrr, and *bang*! I fucking roll away clean! Dude, the super even started clapping! Like, whatever you think about skateboarding, no one can deny the ridiculousness of landing a kickflip five-o down a set of stairs, that's what dreams are made of."

"Wow, congrats! If I knew what it looked like, I'm sure I'd agree."

"That story didn't mean much to you, did it?"

"I enjoyed listening! I think it's the same as when I tell you about my dissertation stuff."

"Huh, right on. Yeah, I don't understand shit about mental realism, but I *do* enjoy when we talk about it."

"Moral relativism. Glad to know it sticks." June laughed.

"That's what books are for, right? They remember words and terms so we don't have to. And moral relativism, it's about how wrong and right only exist as constructs that society dictates? Like the laws of people dictate what is moral?"

"Ay, spot on! And my paper is about?"

"How that's a load of bullshit, that morality exists objectively, and that humans are essentially organic computers moving through a cosmic slop of atoms?"

"Yea! Damn, you do know, Sherm. I'm actually really proud you said that."

"Well, I couldn't ask for a better professor. You wanna watch a movie?"

"Fuck yes I do. *The Hunger*, can you pull it out, please?"

"I thought we might impliment some democracy in the decision, but yeah, sure. What's it about?"

"David Bowie and Susan Sarandon are goth vampires."

Sherm shuffled through the expansive VHS collection while June cheffed up a meal fit to feed a rugby team. The rain subsided to a light spitting rain, and they enjoyed double portions in front of the film.

"Huh, that was strange." Sherm stubbed out the cannoli giganteschi sized dessert spliff.

"Yes." June smiled.

"I'm stuffed." Sherm said, sliding back into the belly of the plush pink couch. "Thank you."

"Me too, I'm gonna take a shower. You staying here tonight?"

"If that's okay?"

"Of course."

"You think Jonny will be back soon?"

"I fucking hope so."

"Can you tell me where you think he is, please?"

June feigned a moment of hard hearing as she dropped their plates in the kitchen, grabbed a tall glass of water, and slunk into the bathroom.

She turned on the shower, drew the curtain, and lifted the toilet seat. With the water running loud, she jettisoned dinner. She downed her glass of water then repeated. She found such pleasure in food, but couldn't stand the weight of it. Her secrecy, her schemeing, and the inability to sit with a meal in her stomach all weighed more, but dysmorphia had deep claws. For over a decade she'd been fighting, and recently she'd been winning, but as she bleached the bowl and cleaned the evidence, she faced the fact that today disorder won.

Every addiction is stoked by the same demon, yet sometimes she wished for a different one. Drink and drugs, you cut all ties, but nobody gets better by quitting food.

"Good shower?" Sherm said as she emerged from a cloud of steam.

"Sure, tomorrow's a new day."

"Huh?"

"Nothing. You want ginger ale?"

"Is it diet?"

"Yep."

"Nah, I'm good, thanks."

June went to pour herself a cup and paused. "Vodka?"

"Hm, why not? Yeah, with ice, please."

June made the drinks, dropped them off at the coffee table, then went to her room to get dressed. She returned to the sofa in black satin sleepwear and clinked glasses with Sherm.

"I realized, I never told you about the cassette tape!"

"What about a cassette tape?"


BANG! A thud hit the front door of the basement. Sherm turned to June, but she was already across the room. She grabbed a metal nightstick from behind the bookshelf and thwacked it to full extension.

"What's going on?" Sherm said, eyes wide and worried.

"I don't know, shush." June turned the corner into the hallway and creeped towards the apartment door. As she drew near, a key fumbled in the lock. Holding her weapon high, she saw Sherm forgot the deadbolt. The doorknob jerked and turned, the door swung slowly open, and there was Jonny doubled over his bicycle.

"Serious?!" June malfunctioned, exasperated. "Are you drunk?"

"No. Fuck, can you help, please?"

"Hold the doorway." June took his bike and wheeled it into the basement. "Sherm! Come get him."

Sherm jumped into action and helped Jonny to the couch. "Dude, what–are you okay?"

"I'll live." He held his face and ribs. "Good looks."

June parked the bike and put on the kettle. "What the fuck!? I fucking told you! Did you listen? No!"

"What's going on?" Sherm's focus darted like a tennis match.

"This fucking idiot–"

"Can you not, please?" Jonny looked up. He spoke through gritted teeth stained bright red. "Yell at me tomorrow, I need you to look at my head."

"Oh fuck!" Sherm pulled back Jonny's hand, his eye was shut tight, his face soaked in blood. "You need to come look at this, June!"

She came over from the kitchen and saw. Jonny had a gash running down his forehead through his brow and terminating beneath his eye. "Shit, lemme go get the kit. Sherm, finish making tea."

"But I–"

"Go make the tea."

June came back to the sofa with a first aid kit, bowl, and wet flannel. "I'm gonna clean this out, disinfect, and stitch you up. Okay?"

"Yea, okay."

June wiped the blood and rainwater from his face, and Jonny moaned when she got close to the cut. "I'm gonna need you to shut the fuck up, alright? It's only getting worse from here." She poured a solution into the bowl, rubber gloved up, and soaked clean strips of fabric in the liquid. "This is gonna sting, hold tight." She held his skin taut with two fingers, and ran the cloth through the wound.

"Arghhh!" Jonny, beat the couch with his fist, still holding tight to his side.

"You're doin' good. Jus' hold still. Think of your guitar scales or some shit."

"It burns, man!"

"I know, but if we don't clean this properly, it's bigger problems down the road."

"Can I–"

"Tea, Sherm! You can help by making us all a cup of tea." June repeated the disinfection process, and proceeded to thread a long curved needle. "Good news is, it missed your eye, barely grazed your cheek. The rain made the blood look crazier than it is. This could'a been a lot worse."

"It hurts pretty bad."

"That's the price of being stupid, huh? Look at me."

Tentatively Jonny opened his left eye, his vision immediately filled with June's piercing stare.

"Si, eyeball is all good. Now, I gotta stitch this shit up."

"Aight, go for it."

"Focus on something, I need you to not move."

"Aeolian, duh, duh, duh…"

"Good, keep with that." June took a deep breath, steadied her hand, and pierced the skin.

"Mixalideon! Ah! Duh, duh, duh…"

"That's it. Don't worry about what I'm doing, jus' sing your little scales." She wove a neat blanket stitch down Jonny's forehead, and continued to reassure him, praising his recital of the various modes.

"Dorian, argh, ah, ah…"

"Nearly there, man." She threaded the needle through his derma one final time and knotted the surgical string. "Done. Leme jus' wipe the blood one more time, and I can patch this up."

With dry clothes and two big band-aids on his face, Jonny sat next to June, and they sipped their tea.

"So what happened, bro?" Sherm said, sitting on the floor opposite the sofa while rolling a spliff on the coffee table.

"It's a long story, dude."

"Pftt!" June made a snarky face. "You put us through all *that*, you better tell us what had happened."

"Aight, I went to Ormen Moving Company."

"What?" Sherm asked.

"OMC, the herald, ah, you don't even—"

"Basically, Ava's letter to Jonny got seized, so he got threatened by a mad man with a machete. In unrelated events he fractured his rib, then he found where the OMC are based, and now he's gone to steal his letter back. Accurate?"

"Yea, sure." Jonny reluctantly endorsed.

"And when did all this happen?"

"Clicked into motion las' night."

"Last night! Dude, I was with you!"

"Got into shit on the train, before the show, then the rest went down today."

"Jheeze, how do you always get into wild situations like this?"

"Do you want the story or not?"

"We want the story. Shut it, Sherm."

"Ai-ight. So boom, I finish band practice–"

"Oh, could we just talk–"

"Sherm, zip!" June's tone left no wiggle room for disobedience.

"So I leave the woodshed, collect some quest items, jump on my bike, and cycle over to Myrtle and Evergreen. Now I'm posted up on Suydam Street, inconspicuous n'shit, on a stoop with a clear view of the front. It's a two story buildin', with a fenced off yard to the side, and an industrial roller door. I staked the place out for a few hours, drained a couple brews, and waited. Now, this shutter thing gotta be opened by hand. I saw a dude raise it from the inside, car drove out, he dropped it, locked it, got in, and drove off. Twenny minutes later, M comes out the buildin' front entrance, tha's the bitch in charge–"

"Language, Jonny."

"Sorry. *La perra* locks up, jumps in the back of a ride, and zoup she's gone."

"Better." June fought against a smile that threatened to betray her stone expression.

"Now I'm thinkin', two goons gone, the boss is done for the day. Shouldn't be no more people in the buildin'. I wait another half hour, for good measure, and no sign of life. All the lights are off, no activity. Thank you." Jonny took the spliff from Sherm and inhaled deeply. "Oooofffff, I needed this. Damn."

"Keep going!" Sherm sanctioned eagerly.

"Aight. So I reckon easiest point of entry is the garage door shits, it's jus' one padlock keepin' it closed. Those two dudes left from there, so I know the yard has access to the buildin'. I threw on my mask, complete the disguise, and grab a spray can from my bag. I jump up on a trash can, and paint over the camera facing the door."

"Can I pause you right there for a sec, on the topic of your outfit. These jeans you had on, what is happening, why are they stapled together?" June looked at the jeans strung over the kitchen chair and drew a circle in the air with her finger. The legs had been cut off above the knee, and crudely reattached with office staples.

"Huh. Yea, so like, I didn't wanna be recognizable. Everyone knows I'm always in shorts, so full length leg coverage, na, that can't be Jonny, ya'know? Those jeans are black, best for a mission, right? Only problem, I made them shorts the day I bought 'em."

"That's not your *only* problem."

"I got the cut-offs, and stapled them back together."

"But where did you get the cut-offs? You've had this pair since before prison."

"I keep'em all. Shoebox under the bed. Seems like a waste to throw away the extra denim."

"That makes sense to me." Sherm concurred.

"Naturally." She said with an undertone of bewildered sarcasm. "Now I'm curious, what else was part of your get-up? What'd you use as a mask?"

"Well, I actually gotta apologize 'bout that, I don't have a regular ski mask so I borrowed yours."

"I don't own a ski mask either."

"Right." Jonny grabbed his backpack and retrieved the mask in question. It was June's black latex hood, now featuring a large rip through the left side.

"What!? Dude, fuck you!"

"What's that?" Sherm asked. "Like a Mexican wrestling mask?"

"No, Mr. Vanilla." June snatched the hood from Jonny. "It's fetish wear, and it's not cheap!"

"I'm sorry, I'll replace it."

"You better! I loved this piece, the eyes are such a nice pointy shape."

"Can I continue?"

"Sure. So you're wearing stapled up jeans, my BDSM mask, and you're painting over the CCTV."

"Yea–actually, also these." Jonny pulled June's leather bike gloves out of his bag. "I couldn't find mine, sorry."

"Puta!" She grabbed them and inspected the damage. "You got red paint on the fuckin' finger tips!"

"I know, kill me mañana. Jus' lemme finish the story so I can go to sleep."

"Fine. Give me that spliff." June commandeered the smoke and gestured for him to commence.

"So camera's taken care of, I get to work on the padlock. Jam a couple wrenches in there, apply some pressure, and pop. Job's a good'un. I slink under the gate into the yard. Now all the ground floor windows are barred up, but I spot one on the second floor tha's open jus' a crack. It's frosted glass, so most likely a toilet window, they prolly airin' that shit out. Still, I needa find a way up. Scopin' out the yard, I check under this tarp, jackpot, I find a fuckin' ladder."

"That's fortunate." Sherm nodded.

"It was. I lean that up against the side of the buildin', climb it, but the window ain't openin' any more. I take a hairclip–" Jonny looked at June, playfully concerned.

"That one I don't mind."

"–and I jimmy the window lock. My first time doin' some shit like that, but it weren't too hard, only had to rotate it a tiny bit to get the latch loose."

"How do you know how to do all this stuff, dude? Like, this is some *real* criminal activity." Sherm scrunched his nose.

"Department of *Connections*, dude. Spend three years talkin' to some *real* criminals, you learn a trick or two."

"Ah, word."

"So window's open, I scramble through. It *was* a toilet, and it fuckin' reeked."

"Irrelevant detail."

"It felt *egregiously* relevant at the time, Bug, and this is my story."

"Solid word, Jonny, egregious."

"Thanks, Germ. *Anyway*, I'm inside. All the lights are out, I flick on my lil' flashlight. Seems like the spot is empty, but I'm sneakin', stealth mode in full effect. I try a couple doors, mainly warehouse shit, jus' a load of boxes. But then I find M's office."

"How did you know it was hers?"

"She had a stellafax machine."

"Woah." Sherm's jaw dropped. "What did it look like?"

"Like something from the future. I thought it would be huge, but this thing was the size of a printer."

"You sure it wasn't jus' a printer?"

"Trus' me, it was *Martian*. Anyway, I search through the desk draws, no sign of her ledger, but I do find a stack of letters."

"Was Ava's letter there?!" Sherm shot up.

"No. But I grab'em all. I knab the stellafax too."

"You got the stellafax?!"

"Chill, I'll get to that. I'm goin' downstairs now, and there's this wild clap of thunder, you heard it?"

"Yeah." They said in unison.

"So I'm tryna make my way to the front door, but this is where shit went left. I guess M's goon was sleepin' there, and the storm woke him up, cause he pops out, wearin' nuttin' but boxer shorts."

"Fuck!"

"Same guy who threatened you?"

"Yea, same guy, and he got the machete on him too. I think M called him Cain on the phone, so le's go with that. Cain's standin' between me and the door, grippin' his blade, sayin' some bullshit 'bout *this his lucky night*. I think 'bout boltin' back up the stairs, but before I getta chance, he jumps toward me, swings down, and I use the stellafax as a shield, hol' that shit above my head. Boaw! Blade connects hard body, sparks flyin' n shit, machete gets lodged in there. He kicks me in the fuckin' chest. I drop the stellafax, hit the deck, I'm all messed up. Cain pulls his knife free, got this sadistic smile on his face, he's enjoyin' the fuck outta it. Man, I thought I was finished. I'm on the floor, he's stood over me, and he said sum' wild like 'let your blood cry from the ground'."

"What the actual fuck."

Jonny breathed deep. "Dude, he swings that shit down, I'm in shock, I don't even try and protect myself. I surrendered to it, forreal, like *this* is my time."

"So h–"

"Shut it, Sherm!"

"Everything moved slow, like a single second went on for eternity. I watch the blade draw down on me, it's 'bouta cleave my head in two. Then–" He paused. "Boom! The front door's kicked off its hinges behind him. These two arms wrap around Cain's stomach like a suplex, and he gets ripped away from me. The machete still swings down though, I feel it slice through my face, jus' tearin' me in two. It hurt so bad I could hear it. My vision's gone red, I hardly see a thing, but I hear Cain scream. I don't know what happened exactly, but adrenaline must'a kicked in big time, cause I pull myself up and stumble to the open door. My ears are ringin' wild, but I hear punch after punch get thrown in the hallway, and Cain ain't makin' no more noise. I fall out into the street, and damn near crawl across the intersection. The rain is comin' down heavy now, and it kinda clears my vision, but I don't even feel like a person at this point. I didn't actually lock my bike up, in case I had'a make a quick getaway, I just draped the chain across it. Good fuckin' thing I did that. I drop the chain, left it behind. I can't ride, not even close. I'm kinda flopped over the frame, jus' usin' it as support, wheelin' myself along. As I'm gettin' the fuck outta there, I see someone leave the buildin', the dude who beat up Cain. All I make out is a silhouette, his face is covered, and he dipped double speed. Now this was more than strange, I swear, blue light beamed from the buildin'. Out the doorway, out every window, jus' whoosh. This crazy flash. I don't look back again. I got 'bout five blocks from there, collapsed. Woke up a while later, soaked and still blind with pain, but I hear sirens. I know I have to move. Drag myself up, slump over the bike, and scoot my way home, felt like a lifetime. I don't even know."

"Christ on a fucking cross, what..."

"Yea." Jonny stared out into nothingness, shell-shocked. "Hard to kill, hard to die."

All June could do was blink.

"I can't, dude–that's the most insane thing I've ever heard! Who was the guy that saved you? Do you think–no! Could it be?"

"The Bully."

"You think so!?"

"How could I know, but who else, man?"

"Wow. And what about the letters? You still have them?"

"Yea, I'm gonna get them back to who they belong to."

"Right on! What do you think the light–"

"I need'a cigarette." June stood up and left the apartment.

She stood on the front patio and puffed. She shook her head, unsure what to make of any of it. Quarter way through the booge, Jonny hobbled out to join her. She exhaled a half-hearted hey.

"Hey." He winced. "Can I bum one?"

She offered the pack and he sparked up.

"I'm sorry, June. For the stuff I wrecked, sure, but I mean, for puttin' you through this."

"Do you have any idea how scared I was tonight?"

"No, I can't imagine."

"I was furious when I got home and you were gone, angry as hell. But then the storm... it was only fear. Fear of losing you."

"Mm, yea. I know thunder–"

"You don't know shit, man. You put yourself at the center of everything, so much so, you don't even realize you do it. You act first, and pick up the pieces after. I do a lot for you, and you throw it back in my face with stunts like this. Why should I take so much care, when you have so little regard for your own life?"

Jonny flinched as he inhaled, and let that sink in.

"Something has to change."

"You're right. I'm sorry."

"No more sorry, we're done with that for tonight. I love you, Jonny."

"Love you too, Bug."


"So this is where the party's at?" Sherm came out to meet them and lit a cigarette of his own. "I go take a leak and you ditch me?"

"We jus' gettin' some air, bro."

"Heard it, heard it. Been a long day."

"The longest." June smirked at Sherm's earnestness.

"You seen this van?" Jonny pointed at The Vando. "That shit's wild. Ain't it exactly the kinda thing you been lookin' for, June?"

"Sí, it's mine." She broke into a smile and Jonny's jaw dropped.

"What? You playin'!"

"Not even nearly. Fancy a quick spin round the block?"

"Mmm. Le'sdoit."

"After that I'm sending you to bed. You gotta get some rest."

"No complaints there."

"You down, Germ?"

"Fuck yes! Just wait one sec, I have the perfect soundtrack."

# Acknowledgements

Thank you for taking the trip! Woodshed is a grassroots project, fuelled by its community, built and published independently. Buying this book directly supports underground artists and helps amplify our collective voice.

This book is written in honour of the friends who died too soon. I hope it can provide comfort to those of us who miss them.

I started writing the storyworld of Woodshed in 2017, and while it's entirely fictional, certain people and experiences have had an immeasurable influence on the characters and narratives.

Among a rich tapestry of collaborators, the first individuals to acknowledge are Mikey, Lembra, and Simeon, who voice the characters of Jonny, June, and Sherm. The escapades and adventures we've shared form the foundation of Woodshed.

Big thanks to Blair, the managing director of Mother Mercury, whose unwavering enthusiasm has been central to the journey of getting this book to print.

Thank you to my incredible partner Chaire, who consistently provides phenomenal input, and unconditional support, even when my book launches the same month as our wedding.

Thank you to my parents for raising me well and providing a life filled with love, art, and literature.

Above all, I thank the gods that guide.

# Mother Mercury

Mother Mercury is an independent publishing company with a focus on feminist, queer, and folk literature. We know that great writing can inspire, empower, and educate readers, so we strive to produce work that represents an inclusive and supportive community. Our passion for storytelling is partnered with a drive for social change, and through the transformative power of language, we aim to help heal, challenge, and activate a global audience. Alongside modern and classic narrative fiction, Mother Mercury publishes 'folkademic' literature that presents accessible non-fiction material, specifically relating to the history and practice of gender, philosophy, magick, and music. We provide a platform for voices that promote a culture of empathy, connection, and creativity through the written word.

Look out for some of our upcoming titles:

# WOODSHED: Apocalaya

The next instalment in the Woodshed series, following on from the events of *Sweet Glass Hearts*, and taking the trip to the furthest bounds of brain-bending post-fantasy fiction.

# THE CITY OF RESURRECTIONS

A collection of sinister stories from the 19th century that examine the corruption of youth against a backdrop of Victorian London. *The City of Resurrections* features *A Child of the Jago*, *The Great God Pan*, and *Confessions of an English Opium-Eater*, accompanied by original introductions & critiques from a range of contemporary writers.

Ollymandias is an author, artist, and musician from North London, working predominantly in the mediums of literary fiction, animation, and audio production. Olly is driven restlessly to create, craft, and tell stories; with a recognised dedication to their artistry, they are an established character of London and New York's underground scenes. They currently work as a visual artist and director within the music industry, professionally collaborating with acts such as Run the Jewels, MF DOOM, and Made Kuti. Their practice combines analog process with a digital toolbox, illustratively bold, and sonically psychedelic. Olly believes in anarchy and the ancient gods; they enjoy playing harmonica and tabletop games.

# WOODSHED

## T-MiNUS

Fresh home from the slammer-jammer clink-klonk Jonny Vulcain picks up the pieces of a life torn by tragedy. Fighting against his fragile grip on reality, the first day at a new job ignites a psychedelic excursion that's sure to test the bounds of his fractured psyche.

# WOODSHED

## ANImatED SeRieS

Watch the Woodshed
animated series at:

WWW.WOODSHED.WORLD
WWW.WOODSHED.WORLD
WWW.WOODSHED.WORLD
WWW.WOODSHED.WORLD
WWW.WOODSHED.WORLD

### MASTERS OF MOJO

### 3D PRINT YOUR OWN JONNY!

Download miniature model files at www.woodshed.world

THE GAME

COMING SOON

NYC *Live Events* LDN

# THOUGHTS? *shout@woodshed.world*

# THE CITY OF RESURRECTIONS

An exerpt from *The Great God Pan*, by Arthur Machen, featured in Mother Mercury's forthcoming title *The City of Resurrections*.

Clarke shivered; the white mist gathering over the river was chilly. "It is wonderful indeed," he said. "We are standing on the brink of a strange world, Raymond, if what you say is true. I suppose the knife is absolutely necessary?"

"Yes; a slight lesion in the grey matter, that is all; a trifling rearrangement of certain cells, a microscopical alteration that would escape the attention of ninety-nine brain specialists out of a hundred. I don't want to bother you with *shop*, Clarke; I might give you a mass of technical detail which would sound very imposing, and would leave you as enlightened as you are now. But I suppose you have read, casually, in out-of-the-way corners of your paper, that immense strides have been made recently in the physiology of the brain. I saw a paragraph the other day about Digby's theory, and Browne Faber's discoveries. Theories and discoveries! Where they are standing now, I stood fifteen years ago, and I need not tell you that I have not been standing still for the last fifteen years. It will be enough if I say that five years ago I made the discovery that I alluded to when I said that ten years ago I reached the goal. After years of labour, after years of toiling and groping in the dark, after days and nights of disappointments and sometimes of despair, in which I used now and then to tremble and grow cold with the thought that perhaps there were others seeking for what I sought, at last, after so long, a pang of sudden joy thrilled my soul, and I knew the long journey was at an end. By what seemed then and still seems a chance, the suggestion of a moment's idle thought followed up upon familiar lines and paths that I had tracked a hundred times already, the great truth burst upon me, and I saw, mapped out in lines of sight, a whole world, a sphere unknown; continents and islands, and great oceans in which no ship has sailed since a man first lifted up his eyes and beheld the sun, and the stars of heaven, and the quiet earth beneath. You will think this all high-flown language, Clarke, but it is hard to be literal. And yet; I do not know whether what I am hinting at cannot be set forth in plain and lonely terms. For instance, this world of ours is pretty well girded now with the telegraph wires and cables; thought, with something less than the speed of thought, flashes from sunrise to sunset, from north to south, across the floods and the desert places. Suppose that an electrician of today were suddenly to perceive that he and his friends have merely been playing with pebbles and mistaking them for the foundations of the world; suppose that such a man saw uttermost space lie open before the current, and words of men flash forth to the sun and beyond the sun into the systems beyond, and the voice of articulate-speaking men echo in the waste void that bounds our thought. As analogies go, that is a pretty good analogy of what I have done; you can understand now a little of what I felt as I stood here one evening; it was a summer evening, and the valley looked much as it does now; I stood here, and saw before me the unutterable, the unthinkable gulf that yawns profound between two worlds, the world of matter and the world of spirit; I saw the great empty deep stretch dim before me, and in that instant a bridge of light leapt from the earth to the unknown shore, and the abyss was spanned. You may look in Browne Faber's book, if you like, and you will find that to the present day men of science are unable to account for the presence, or to specify the functions of a certain group of nerve-cells in the brain. That group is, as it were, land to let, a mere waste place for fanciful theories. I am not in the position of Browne Faber and the specialists, I am perfectly instructed as to the possible functions of those nerve-centers in the scheme of things. With a touch I can bring them into play, with a touch, I say, I can set free the current, with a touch I can complete the communication between this world of sense and—we shall be able to finish the sentence later on. Yes, the knife is necessary; but think what that knife will effect. It will level utterly the solid wall of sense, and probably, for the first time since man was made, a spirit will gaze on a spirit-world. Clarke, Mary will see the god Pan!"

Milton Keynes UK
Ingram Content Group UK Ltd.
UKHW010726151123
432615UK00004B/198